The E Collection

TERRY B. is the penname for Terry William Benjamin and
Tobias Ariel Fox

Also by Terry W. Benjamin and Tobias A. Fox under their
penname Terry B.:

Fiction

Dancer's Paradise: An Erotic Journey
At Midnight: Choice Fowler's Story

Memoir

Keith Lynch with (Tobias A. Fox using the penname) Terry B.:

Dirty Justice: Who Killed Mommy

A New Definition of *Erotica*

TERRY B.

nHouse Publishing, L.L.C.

Newark

This is a work of fiction. Names, characters, places and incidents either are the product of the author's imagination or are used fictitiously, and any resemblance to actual persons, living or dead, business establishments, events, or locales is entirely coincidental.

nHouse Publishing, L.L.C.
P.O. Box 1038
Newark, New Jersey 07101
973-223-9135
www.nhousepublishing.com

The ℰCollection
Volume 1 published 2007
ISBN 10-digit 0-9726242-2-8
ISBN 13-digit 978-0-9726242-2-0
Library of Congress Catalog Number: 2007906742
   1. Erotica, Women, Hip-Hop, African American,
       Multicultural, Contemporary – Fiction

Cover and book design by www.mariondesigns.com
Photograph by Akintola Hanif (www.akintolahanif.com)
Edited by Carla M. Dean (www.ucanmarkmyword.com)

Printed in Canada

MEMO

FROM: The Desk of Terry B.

TO: Our Readers

SUBJECT: Erotica with a Twist

DATE: The Future

Submitted for your approval is the best erotic fiction from the dynamic duo that brought you the bestselling novels *Dancer's Paradise: An Erotic Journey* and *At Midnight: Choice Fowler's Story.* We offer you great stories, interesting characters, and literary content without cheating you, the reader.

Even though erotica is the bestselling genre of contemporary literature, Terry B. understands that there is a higher and deeper level that has not yet been explored. Thanks to the groundbreaking work of writers like Mary B. Morrison, Zane, and Eric Jerome Dickey erotica is no longer a derogatory word or something to avoid. Readers worldwide look forward to the latest and the best in this genre. Still, the question remains: what is next?

Terry B. has the answer: *The E Collection Volume 1* (E for *Erotica*), a multi-cultural and erotic read with the emphasis on human experience. In this collection you will enter the intimate lives of a cast of characters that will make you feel like the voyeur you always wanted to be.

Yes, with these stories you can be that fly on the wall, taking it all in and saying, "My, my, my I can't believe they went there with that!"

The E *Collection* is for those broad minded people who realize that the mind is the biggest sex organ, the body does react, and the spirit is fed with many pleasurable and memorable sensations.

Please let us know what you think about this one, so that we can give you more of what you really want in your erotic fiction, because like the best lover you ever had, Terry B. is ever ready and more than willing to please.

Be on the lookout for *The* E *Collection Volume 2,* coming very soon.

Contents

A Love Journey

The moon illuminated the sky on this cool summer night. The evening coming to an end, we were driving in my car with the windows down, listening to cuts by John Legend, 112, Common, Usher, and Mariah Carey. My date seemed to be feeling Mariah's "We Belong Together," but I was contemplating my next move while tapping my fingers on the steering wheel.

"I really enjoyed our night out," I finally said.

"Me, too," Journey replied, breaking her concentration from the music to give me her full attention.

We smiled as John Legend's "Ordinary People" broke through the airwaves. I really did enjoy the movie and dinner, even though I was more into her than what was playing on the big screen. Next time, I would prefer dinner and a movie at my place. This way I could show her that I have some skills in the kitchen. Or maybe we could go out dancing at Club Cherries in Atlanta so I can see how she moves her body on the dance floor and show off my fancy footwork.

"We should do it again some time…soon," I said.

"I'd like that."

Thoughts were racing through my mind. We were back at my place, and I had to think fast. She had driven her car to my house, but we agreed to go on our date in my ride. Now we were both waiting to say goodbye. Looking at my watch, I noticed the time…12:25 A.M.

The night is still young, I thought.

We had learned so much about one another in just a single night. Journey Love, originally from Birmingham, Alabama, is the older of two siblings with aspirations of being something larger than life, unlike her mother and father. I saw sorrow in her eyes, even tears she fought back while telling me about her childhood. Understanding her pain, I felt compelled to tell her my life story of how I grew up in East Orange and Newark, New Jersey, where it's overpopulated with drugs, crime, and gangs. The grass definitely wasn't greener on either side. As I saw it, we were a match made in Augusta, Georgia, where we now lived.

We'd met two weeks ago at the Cheesecake Factory. I bumped into her while she was coming out and I was going in. After our apologies and becoming somewhat acquainted, we exchanged numbers.

Common's song "Go" came on next and pumped me with courage. "Look, Journey, I really don't want this night to end just yet. Why don't you come inside?"

"Okay," she answered after a short delay in response. "I can stay for a little while."

I tried hard to keep my composure and be the perfect gentleman. They say the first impression is a lasting impression, so you should make it the best, which is what I was aiming to do. At the end of this night, I didn't want to have to worry about whether or not I would hear from her again.

After making our way to my front door and stepping inside, Journey walked deeper into my place and entered the living room. I came up behind her and asked, "Do you want something to drink?"

"No," she answered while taking off the light jacket she'd been wearing to cover her bare arms while we were in the theatre. Her Chanel perfume quickly filled the air and stirred my emotions, like fuel to my fire. *Damn, she's gorgeous,* was all I could think as I stood facing her.

"Can I get you anything?" I asked.

"No, I'm good."

"Would you like to hear some music then?"

"Sure," Journey said as she sat down on the couch.

I walked over to the entertainment system, hit the power button, and cued 112's "U Already Know." As the sound of music broke the silence, I cleared my mind and thought, *What the hell.* Walking back over to Journey full of confidence, I took her by the hand, pulled her up off the couch, and snuggled her close to my body.

"This is something I wanted to do all day," I confessed, and then pressed my lips against hers.

It seemed like we were kissing forever. We started out with small pecks, which led to wet, passionate kisses as our tongues danced. She occasionally sucked on my bottom lip and I returned the pleasure. The pounding rhythms of our heartbeats drowned out the sounds coming from the speakers. We were speaking a body language only she and I could understand. We were in a world of our own, letting everything go. Then I felt her body pulling back, and I followed suit as we came up for air.

God, I want this woman, I thought.

She was every bit of a woman, and not just in a physical sense. The way she carried and expressed herself assured me she had stopped being a little girl a long time ago, and that turned me on even more. What I like most about Journey, though, was she showed a genuine interest in me. She actually paid attention when I spoke, as if everything I said mattered. How could I just let her go? I wanted her. No, I *had* to have her.

"Let's go in the bedroom," I seductively suggested, trying not to sound demanding or controlling, but wanting to know everything there was to know about Journey's love.

I took her silence as a yes. After turning off the music, I took Journey by the hand and led her into my bedroom. Once inside, I didn't bother turning on the lights. Instead, I lit a candle and turned on my satellite radio, which was tuned to the slow jam station. As K-C and Jo-Jo crooned "Stay," I noticed the time on my digital clock…12:45 A.M.

It's still pretty early considering the night, I thought.

I turned to Journey, who stood by the door anticipating my next move. As I passed her to close the door, my body brushed against hers. I wanted to warn her anything goes behind this closed door, but I'm sure the expression on my face told her that I was going to take pleasing her very seriously.

The shadows from our bodies touched before we did. Our spirits connected. Our minds were in sync the entire evening. Now, it was time to find out how well we would respond physically to one another.

She wasted no time as she placed her hand behind the back of my head, pulling me closer to her. We kissed again, but this time with a heated passion I never felt before. Journey and I had become completely different people from just moments ago. It was like the soft music and burning of the candle helped set the mood for this love scene. However, there was no director, no script, and we definitely weren't actors.

As we kissed, we started pulling and tugging at each other's clothes. In the process, we stumbled into the wall, the door, and against the dresser, knocking over the contents sitting on top. We were acting like two drunken, lovesick fools. Yet,

neither one of us had anything to drink. In that sense, we were

actors, but everything we did was adlib, just going with the flow

of things. We continued this wild dance until we were completely

naked.

Our breathing was heavy, hearts racing as we stood

fully exposed, facing one another. We no longer cared what was

playing on the radio. There were no embarrassing moments. No

awkwardness. No shame in our game. We knew what we wanted

and how we wanted it.

Still, I had to make the first move to protect my ego, to

feel in control of this intense situation. She must've sensed this

because she complied and let me lead her three steps to my queen

size bed.

"Do you have protection?" she asked.

I walked over to the nightstand, opened the drawer, and

pulled out a pack of three…Magnum, of course. After stepping

back over to Journey, we both climbed onto the bed. I lay on my

back, placing the condoms by my side, and then pulled her on

top. Journey thought I wanted her to ride me, but I had other plans. She looked at me strangely as I tried to pull her up further.

"I want to taste you," I said in a seductive whisper.

Knowing exactly what I was talking about, Journey crawled up my body and even purred like a kitten, but I knew better. I knew once she got open, she would become a wild alley cat. She didn't stop climbing until her bottom was above my face. As she spread her legs, her pussy smiled and I could see the moistness on her clit, aiming for my mouth. I licked my lips on cue as she lowered herself.

I opened my mouth and accepted all she had to offer. As I sucked and pulled on her clitoris, my bottom lip slid in and out of her. I looked up and saw that Journey had her eyes closed. Her head fell back, then to the side, and then forward, as if she had no control over her body. She licked her lips as she rubbed and stroked her breasts and nipples. She was in her zone, enjoying every sensual pleasure of having her clitoris stimulated.

She then became forceful, grabbing my head with both hands and riding my mouth like a go-go dancer giving a lap dance. All I could do was grab her waist, hold on, and enjoy the ride. Her juices flooded my mouth as she began moving faster, and faster, and faster.

"Come on, baby. Get this pussy. Get this pussy. You want it? Tell me you want it."

I tried responding, but the wider I opened my mouth the deeper she pushed herself in. I was drowning in her love. Suddenly, her body started jerking and tightening up.

"I'm...about...to...come, baby!"

Her words and reaction excited me. I even tried doing a little head movement to enhance her orgasm, but it was useless. She used my head like a sex toy. A flood of emotions overflowed my mouth as her juices ran down the sides of my face. Journey jerked her body back as she began moaning and screaming, creating a soundtrack of her own. She pounded her fist against the headboard before collapsing on my face.

She tried to regain her strength and composure while lifting up and sliding down onto my body. As I looked into her eyes, I saw tears flowing down her cheeks. Not knowing what to say, I said nothing.

"I'm sorry, baby," she said with all sincerity. "I needed that."

You really never know what one is going through, I thought.

Journey hugged and kissed me on the lips, but didn't stop there. She started kissing on my neck and chest, giving my nipples special attention, which really got me aroused. I arched my back a little and let out a deep moan of my own. Journey smiled as she continued teasing me, as if she liked seeing me in such a vulnerable state.

She moved down to my belly button and then put all of me inside her mouth, giving me some deep throat action. This caused my toes to curl and my back to arch more than normal. My mouth fell open, but nothing that came out made sense, only sounds. I grabbed onto my sheets as if I was on a dangerous ride and didn't want to fall off. Emotions were building up inside of me and a knot was forming in my stomach.

What's happening, I wondered.

I became scared and pushed Journey off of me.

"What's wrong?" she asked, sounding concerned.

"Nothing."

I had to stay in control. I didn't want to lose control.

"Lay on your back," I demanded, but my forcefulness

only made Journey smile as she complied.

I put on a Magnum condom and climbed on top of Journey, whose legs were spread wide open. She was wet and ready. I slid in and out of her in slow motion at first, and then sped things up a bit. I lifted her legs, arched myself in a pushup position, and turned it into a workout session. After about a set of fifty, I put Journey's legs down, placed my legs outside of hers, and began climbing up the ladder. I pushed myself as deep as I could go inside her.

Journey kept challenging me to go deeper, faster, harder, and I tried my best to stay in the game. She definitely was picking up what I was putting down. She scratched the flesh of my back as she moaned deeply in my ear.

Pulling myself out, I said, "Turn over. I want it from the back."

Journey kept smiling, taunting and teasing my ego. She got on all fours, resting the top of her body on the bed while reaching back to spread her cheeks.

"Come get this pussy, daddy."

That I did. I slid inside her, gently pulling her hair and

kissing her softly on her neck as I went in and out, in and out, in and out. She kept encouraging me, letting me know I was performing to her satisfaction.

"Come on, baby. Don't stop! Don't stop!"

I kept this rhythm going until Journey's walls erupted and there was an explosion once again. Her body collapsed on the bed and I rested mine on top of hers while still inside. I then got up and turned over onto my back. I looked over at the clock and saw it was 2:00 A.M. We had been going at it for about an hour strong. I smiled, proud of my stamina and self control.

"My turn now, baby. Get on top of me."

Journey used every bit of strength she had left and pulled her body on top of mine. She smiled, obviously impressed at how I was able to keep up.

"You gonna come for me, baby?" she asked.

I just smiled back.

Journey grabbed my dick with one hand as she squatted and positioned herself. Then she dropped down and did The Eagle. She moved in a circular motion as she rested her hands on my chest. We moved in unison. Our bodies became one. We created a dance of our own. It was a dirty dance, a downright funky dance. We began moving faster, and I felt a tingling at the head of my dick.

"I'm about to come! I'm about to come!" I shouted.

"Yes, baby, let it go. Please, don't hold back."

I released everything I had in me. The emotions once built up inside of me returned, and so did the knot in my stomach. I couldn't hold back any longer. I had to release it all.

Journey leaned down and kissed me on my hot, wet face. I noticed a strange look on her face, as if she was holding something back, but wanted to get it out. Then, tears started to fall from her eyes. However, she smiled and this confused me even more. It was as if she was sad and happy all at the same time.

"What's wrong?" I asked.

She leaned in closer and whispered, "Baby, you're crying. I never saw a man so emotional after sex."

Crying? Me? I never felt this emotion before. I never cried during sex. I felt embarrassed, ashamed. I tried wiping the tears from my eyes, but they wouldn't go away. I was crying for sure. And then it all poured out. I cried like a baby and held on to

Journey as if my life depended on it.

Once You Go Black

Dear Hillary,

After it was all over, I didn't want to get out of the bed.
Even though we had gone at it hot and heavy that night, it still
wasn't enough for me. I greedily wanted more, more, and more.
To say he blew my mind is an understatement. With that man,
that lover, the earth moved and the stars fell from the sky. The
scary thing is I almost missed this opportunity by being my
conservative self.

"I don't deal with conservative women," I overheard him
say as I came out of the ladies' room. We were at a university-wide
celebration and the administration went all out with the food and
drinks. I walked pass him and a small group of men who were
drinking and trash talking, like they had to prove that although
they were intellectual men, college professors and administrators,
they were still virile men that screwed women.

Blushing, I turned beet red because I knew he was talking

about sex with a woman like me. Although I had eavesdropped, I knew the only way we could get together was if I changed my conservative ways and didn't block an opportunity for a most excellent sexual experience. But only if I were ready and willing to take that chance.

He stood tall and manly in his black tuxedo with silk purple lapels. I thought his tux was a little flashy for this conservative crowd. Because he was a young, black college professor, I couldn't expect him to dress or even act like the old heads that had been around when I was an undergraduate at Florida University where we both worked.

Since I got a lot of compliments from men and women on my peach and cream silk gown, I guess I wasn't looking too shabby myself. The gown swept the floor, covering my peach and cream silk pumps, and he almost stepped on the bottom of it as we danced to the music of the live band that consisted of undergraduate music majors.

He taught African American Literature and I taught Political Science. I never imagined we would even be at the same table, but because I decided to attend the banquet at the last

him, but I needed a little more information. "Who told you this, Gayle?"

"A sistah who ran into him recently at a party. She laid some not-so-subtle hints on the brotha, but he didn't respond at all. Then, this white woman shows up and he practically runs to greet her. How ya like that?"

To me, that didn't seem like enough to label him a lover of white women exclusively. My feeling was that a man, black or white, who respected a woman made her feel special around him. All I saw him being was a respectable gentleman.

"He also doesn't like conservative women," Gayle went on, telling me something I had already heard from his mouth. I just wasn't sure what *she* meant by it.

"Conservative, Gayle?"

"In bed. Too conservative. Too uptight when it comes to certain things."

"Certain things like what?" I naively asked.

Gayle looked at me like I was crazy. "He likes his dick sucked and his balls licked. A lot of sistahs don't get down freaky like that."

"And he likes white woman because they do all that?"
I asked, amused by such stereotyping in this day and age. I am
a thirty-four-year-old white woman and before that particular
night I had never licked any man's testicles. To tell the truth, I
was afraid to touch them, stroke them, or fondle them, fearing I
might hurt the man and it would be such a turn off that he would
never want to have sex with me again. Whenever the thought
of something "freaky" like that crossed my mind, I dismissed it
because I felt the next thing my lover would want me to do was
ream his ass crack with my tongue. And that was something a
conservative like me would never do. It was like going where no
man (or woman) had ever gone before. I had to shake my head
and wonder where she got those crazy ideas about white women.

Gayle looked at me like she expected some confirmation.

"I can't speak for all white women," I told her, "but,
Gayle, not all white women do those things in bed."

Gayle looked at me skeptically. "Suck dick, lick balls,
and take it up the ass," she said as if to sum up the full sexual
repertory of white American women.

I could've told her that I sucked cock, but never took

it up the shitter. I always thought of my rectum as an exit, not an entrance. Maybe I was being too conservative in this new millennium.

"Are you uncomfortable with this conversation?" Gayle asked, obviously commenting on my sudden silence.

"It's not that," I assured her, groping for a satisfactory answer to her question. "I'm not uncomfortable with discussions about sex. It's just all this talk about sexual preferences may be a speculation, Gayle. I don't know him like that and neither do you…I mean, we don't know him intimately."

"I've heard a lot of things, though."

"Okay, but have you ever been there with him, Gayle?"

"I wish. I would let him tap this ass."

I couldn't help but to blush.

Gayle laughed out loud, a low sexy growl. That sexy low laugh seemed to come from somewhere between Gayle's thighs. It was a cross between a moan and a whimper. The thought of such deep carnality pulled my thoughts away from the professor for a moment and had me thinking about the first time I did something sexual that I was totally unprepared for. And because I was totally unprepared for it, I didn't enjoy it as much as I could have.

Even though Gayle said black women were not his first choice, I couldn't help but imagine the two of them together, screwing their brains out and sweating like pigs, their dark bodies on white satin sheets while her heels were up on his broad shoulders and his dark brown cock pumped into her tight, wet cunt. I had to admit Gayle had me thinking sexy thoughts about the professor.

"I bet he's got a nice, big, juicy dick, too," Gayle continued, obviously intoxicated from the champagne.

I was glad when he returned to the table because I didn't want to engage in any more sex talk with Gayle Lord, especially when I had come to the banquet hall alone and planned to go home alone. Why get my cunt all wet when there was no one to satisfy me? I could do the job myself, but I had never been a fan of solo sex. After an orgasm, I like pillow talk. You couldn't get that from a sex toy.

The evening came to an end with brief remarks from the president of the university. While making my way out of the banquet hall and into the parking lot, he called out to me.

"Diane," the professor called as I stood near my Lexus.

"Can I help you?" I asked, a lot more formal than I intended to be. I felt like I had to protect myself, to resist the charm of this black man who only bedded white women. Still, I blushed, my face hot because of my presumptuousness. Who was I to think he wanted me naked with my legs spread wide just because I was a white woman?

"You can *help* Gayle," he answered with a killer smile, brilliant white teeth, and healthy pink gums. "I don't think Gayle is in any shape to drive herself home."

"You want me to drive her home?" I asked, wanting to make sure I understood his request.

"That's right," he told me. "I want you to drive Gayle in your car and I'll drive Gayle's car. That way, Gayle won't have to leave it here in the parking lot."

"How did you get here tonight?" I asked out of curiosity.

"Public transportation. I had no idea I would be here tonight. The chairman of my department had some extra tickets; he gave me one for free and said it would be good politics if I showed my face."

I nodded, letting him know I understood all about departmental and university politics. I had many collegiate war stories of my own that I could share with him.

"Besides, as a new professor, I can't afford the luxury of a car."

I nodded again. I knew starting out on your own always contained some element of struggle.

We went back into the banquet hall and found Gayle in the ladies' room puking her guts out. Well, it would be more accurate to say *I* found her in the ladies' room, and he waited outside the door.

Gayle seemed glad to see me as she hugged the commode like it was a long lost friend. The miracle for me was she didn't get any puke on her gown. I helped her to her feet. Outside the ladies' room, she used me and the professor as crutches while the three of us made it out to the parking lot. She handed the professor her car keys, and he followed behind me in her car.

Gayle rode with me, sprawled out across the backseat. Once we arrived at her apartment and settled her in the bed, we got back on the road.

"Where to?" I asked.

He gave me directions to his apartment and we were there in less than fifteen minutes.

"You look beautiful tonight," he expressed as we sat in front of his apartment building.

"Thank you," I replied, and then blushed.

"I know it's late, so I won't keep you," he told me while unbuckling his seatbelt.

"You're not keeping me from anything."

"I can't believe Gayle got blasted like that," he said, having no idea he played a role in Gayle's overindulgence.

"You had something to do with it."

"Me? How?"

"I shouldn't be telling you this, but Gayle has a major crush on you."

He looked shocked. "Gayle never said anything to me, Diane. We didn't even have any small talk until you came to join us. I just sat there in silence while Gayle drank glass after glass of champagne. You saw her; she didn't even touch her food. A crush on me? How could that be?"

"Don't ask me to explain it fully, but my guess is that Gayle finds you intimidating."

He laughed out loud. "Intimidating? Me? I'm a pussycat."

"That's the only way I can account for her shyness."

"So because she can't talk to me, Gayle drinks too much, gets sick, and embarrasses herself?"

"Like I said, I can't fully explain it, but that is my take on the situation."

He shook his head in wonderment as if to say, *I don't understand women at all.*

"Besides that, Gayle thinks you prefer white women over black women."

"Where'd she get that crazy idea?"

Then I was a little puzzled. "You don't prefer white women as lovers?"

"Diane, read my lips. I've *never* been with a white woman sexually."

"That's what Gayle believes, which is another reason for her to think she doesn't have a chance with you."

"Next, you're going to tell me that she believes white women are better in bed than black women."

I held up my hands in mock surrender. "I don't want to get into that debate. I have no field evidence to refute that proposition."

He smiled broadly. "No 'field evidence'? Are you telling me that everything can be proven by field evidence?"

"A lot of my distinguished colleagues swear by it."

"What about you?"

"I get a lot of good information from libraries and the Internet."

"But is it ever as satisfying as tracking down 'field evidence'?"

I found myself blushing and becoming aroused at the same time. I felt he was manipulating me, and I didn't like that at all.

"Don't push me into a corner on this," I snapped. "I'm just trying to help you understand Gayle. Don't push me like this. I don't like to be manipulated in any way."

"Is that what I'm doing?" he asked defensively.

"I detect some not-so-subtle sexual probing."

"Diane, are you saying I'm trying to turn you on? I mean, because it's a known fact that I like white women so much."

"I think we should end this discussion right now," I said, feeling that he was teasing me a little too much. As far as I was concerned, he was dismissed, but it was obvious he didn't see it that way. He made no move to exit my car. I couldn't see pushing this young man away, especially when he smelled the erotic possibility of some white cunt.

"I've never been with a white woman," he repeated, as if he expected me to do something about that oversight, like I was part of some "field evidence" he wanted to gather. "Have you ever had a black man, Diane?"

Before I could answer, he kissed me so hard and fast my head spun and my panties became instantly wet.

With some reluctance, I managed to push him away. "I'm not conducting any research here," I let him know, trying hard to sound indignant. He had no right asking me such a question and absolutely no right putting his lips on me. I pushed myself away from him. "I'm not about to serve you my cunt in the interest of research."

"Is that so?" he said as he moved toward me.

It was almost as if, in spite of my protest, he could see how much I wanted his cock buried inside me. I never had a black man, but everything he said and did made me want him more and more. Still, I didn't want to be considered "easy."

That's why when he came within striking distance, I slapped him hard across his smirking face. I surprised him, but it didn't stop him. He just grabbed my shoulders and kissed me again, this time thrusting his tongue between my lips. Soon, I was moaning with my tongue dueling with his.

"Your place or mine?" he asked when he finally took his tongue out of my mouth. I had to admit I wanted more.

"Your place," I said breathlessly, "but only because we're already here."

I'm giving my cunt to a black man, I thought while exiting my car.

I walked a little ahead of him as we entered the apartment building. In the elevator, standing so close to his masculinity, I felt small at five-five and barely one hundred and ten pounds. As we rode up to the twenty-third floor, I couldn't help but wonder if he would like my 34-25-36 figure.

Inside his bachelor apartment, he flicked on the lights. The sparsely furnished living room had a fresh, clean soft pine scent permeating the air, as if he was expecting company that evening. However, I quickly replaced that thought with admiration; he was just a young man who kept a neat apartment.

Before following him into his bedroom, I kicked off my pumps in the living room. Once inside, I found it to also be neat and sparsely furnished. He went over to a mini-music entertainment center as I reached under my gown to pull down my sheer white pantyhose. When my legs were bare, I rolled up my pantyhose and put them atop his long dresser. Suddenly, the bedroom was filled with the soothing sounds of Luther Vandross. I didn't know many R&B singers, but I knew Luther, thanks to you, Hillary.

Reaching out, he grabbed me and pulled me into his arms. I felt light as he moved my body in tune with the soft, romantic music. I really wanted to talk to him, to let him know I wasn't some loose white woman, but that I was with him because the essence of his style and manner had captivated me.

There I was about to climb into his bed because everything felt so right. I didn't want him to think I was putting out just because he was a black man and I had *jungle fever*. However, I said none of this as we danced.

Because he had removed the jacket of his tux, I was able to run my hands up and down the front of his white silk tuxedo shirt. Still, that wasn't enough for me. I unbuttoned his shirtfront, then reached inside to massage his hot flesh. I opened his shirt wider, then bent to suck on his dark nipples. I moaned and groaned because as I teased him with my mouth, his big hands massaged my hot behind.

It was I who pushed him away, not able to stand anymore sweet torture of our foreplay. "Please," I begged, "let's take everything off."

It was almost like a race to see who would get naked first. I won and quickly climbed into his bed. I watched intently as he pushed down his boxer shorts. With him still standing, I reached out for his stiff cock. Rubbing it between my hot palms, I was amazed at the rigid smoothness of it. As I took him into my mouth, he reached down to massage my cunt lips.

"So wet," he remarked as he stuck two fingers inside me.

He had me squirming all over the bed. I felt like the hot white woman of his dreams as he made me burn and cream for him, the flow from my cunt embarrassing as he shamelessly fondled me.

"I've got to have you inside me," I told him as I pulled him on top of me. When he pushed his big cock inside of me, I threw my legs up so they rested on his shoulders. I reached down to feel his cock as he ran in and out of me.

"Screw me! Screw me hard!" I screamed as I bounced my ass up and down on his bed.

The sight of his dark brown cock disappearing in my dusky pink cunt took me over the edge. I groaned as my cunt clenched and released over his hot stiffness. My legs trembled as I lost all control.

Then he grunted and came inside me.

"You're too much," I said while snuggling close to him, his naked body covered by a single sheet, my naked body too hot to be covered by anything. I just couldn't get enough of his hands on me, especially on my hot behind that had become one big erogenous zone, a creamy white behind I wanted him to fondle and lick.

My hand searched under the sheet until I found his magnificent cock, still thick, but soft now. He had shot a mighty load in me.

"I want you again," I told him. "I want you hard and inside me again."

"I have to rest a bit."

"I can get you hard again," I boldly told him, wanting him urgently inside of me. I trembled with my need for him. I whispered softly as I threw my bare leg across his thigh. "This hot, white woman wants you inside her so bad. So damn bad, baby."

"I want you, too. I really do," he replied as I moved to kneel between his wide spread legs.

"I'll tell you a story, a nice hot story to get you hard."

He laughed like there was no story I could tell that would get his cock hard for me.

"You asked me if I had ever had a black man," I said while holding his cock with one hand and tickling his balls with the other.

"And you never answered me."

"Does it matter?"

"I'm just curious."

"You want to know if I had another black man's cock inside me."

"Only if you want to tell me."

"You think I'd just let any man, black or white, screw me like this?"

"How would I know?"

"Would the thought of another black man being inside me turn you on?"

"I'm just curious, Diane. No big deal, really."

"You want to know if I sucked his cock like I sucked your cock? If I licked his balls like I licked your balls?"

"Only if you want to tell me."

"After the time we had, you know I'll tell you everything you want to know. I know I'll be sore tomorrow morning because of the way I indulged myself. Still, I want you stiff and big inside me."

"I don't think that's going to happen tonight, Diane. Perhaps in the morning before we leave."

"I want you now, and you *will* get real hard once I tell you my story, Professor."

"The story of you with another black man?"

"I've never been with another black man; you are my first. But I have been with a black woman."

That's when I told him about you, Hillary.

"A professor that once worked at the university," I began, my head resting on his chest, my hand wrapped around his cock. "We went to a conference in Greensboro, North Carolina, representing the university. I believe they sent us because she said we wouldn't have a problem sharing a room. I drew the line at sharing a bed, but the room was big with two queen beds. Since most of our time was taken up with seminars and symposiums, we had very little time for any sightseeing, but we did do some fun stuff, like shopping at the mall and seeing comedian Chris Rock in concert at War Memorial Auditorium.

"I had a ball and Professor Hillary Boston got to see another side of me, my backside. Or at least that's what she noticed when we got back to our hotel room. She told me how nice my backside looked in the dark blue tailored slacks I wore. She told me most white women she met had flat behinds and was somewhat surprised by the roundness of mine. I giggled, somewhat giddy from our drinks after the concert. I can't remember whose idea it was to compare behinds. Somehow, I don't think it was mine; I don't think I could ever be that bold.

"Hillary wore a short skirt and lifted it to show off what she called her 'big black ass.' But I didn't see it as too big or too black. She is a light-skinned black woman, and her behind was the color of coffee with a lot of creamer added. Because she wore a thong, her behind was fully exposed.

"Things got real crazy when Hillary suggested I remove my slacks so she could get a good look at my behind. Still giggling, and not believing what I was doing, I turned away and dropped my slacks to my ankles. But that wasn't enough for Hillary. She asked me to pull down my panties so she could see my entire behind. I posed for her and even shook it a little in her face. At the time, I thought it was fair, considering she showed me all of her behind. I sat on my bed as Hillary removed her skirt

and pulled down her thong. Bare like that, it looked even bigger
and rounder, the cleft between her cheeks even deeper.

"As she stood there with her hands on her round hips, I
shyly touched her behind. I guess you could blame it on the wine.
I found it to be butter soft, and because she didn't seem freaked
out by another woman touching her, I used both my hands. It
was a good minute or so of behind rubbing before Hillary excused
herself and went into the bathroom.

"I got real nervous because I thought I had gone too
far. I was sitting on the bed, my behind still bare, when Hillary
came out of the bathroom. My first thought was to apologize for
the liberties I had taken with her hot, ripe, womanly body. But
because she came out of the bathroom naked, I didn't feel there
was anything to apologize for. She told me that I had gotten
her wet. Then using two hands, she opened herself for me and
showed how wet I had gotten her. She stood so close to me that I
could smell her arousal.

"I reached out to touch between her thighs, and stroked
her thick black bush while massaging my own wet cunt. She
held onto my wrist as I shoved my fingers in and out of her hot

wetness. I moaned loudly when her hands cupped my breasts. Her legs were spread wide as she removed my top and bra. When she fell on top of me, I fell back onto the bed and spread my legs wide, too. Her hands roamed from my neck, to my belly, to my cunt. Of course, I wanted more of her. Showing some athleticism, Hillary moved her long, thick body so that her hot behind was in my face and her face was between my thighs. We ate each other out until we screamed, trembled, and climaxed."

Needless to say, at the end of my story, the professor's cock was rock hard. And since I was so crazy with need, I gave him what I thought he expected from a white woman. Because I had given everything else, I felt there was only one last thing to give. I got down on all fours in the bed and let him know there was nothing I would deny him, my first black man. As he took me like that, all I could say was, "Your big cock feels so good in my ass."

I am writing this as I sit in my condo, alone. He called me this Monday morning after our great weekend, our unreal weekend. He called me from the university, concerned because I called in sick. I just couldn't get out of bed. I only wanted to lounge around and think about us. With no shame, I told him that I couldn't wait to see him again, that my body ached for him. He asked if I had made up the story of being with a black woman. I laughed because only you and I know how very true that story is.

Being with him has made the memories of you and I even sweeter. It also brought back to my mind something you said as we were coming back on the plane from Greensboro. I didn't know how true those words were at that time.

You said, and I quote, "Once you go black, you never go back."

Yours truly,
Diane

Computer Love

We met two months ago on Black Planet (BP), an online dating
website. After conducting a search for women in the age group
of twenty-five to twenty-nine living in New Jersey, the username
MsDrippingWet immediately caught my attention. Expecting an
erotic web page, I was surprised to find it wasn't. Instead, it was
just a simple headshot with a little information describing her.

*Hello out there on BP. You've dropped in on MsDrippingWet,
and I would like to thank you for stopping by. Just a little something
about me: I stand about five feet six inches and weigh in at a lovely…
wait, I don't know you well enough to tell, but let's just say I wear it
well. I'm a workaholic; however, I will come out to play if the purpose
is right, but if it's not, I keep it moving. I'm not a chef, but a pretty
mean sistah in the kitchen. (LOL) Also, I take pride in my physical
appearance, so I workout regularly.*

*If you'd like to learn more, drop me a note, but don't leave
without signing my guestbook. Show a sistah some love, as I will*

truly do the same. Oh yeah, if you don't have a pic, don't expect me to respond.

Her bio provided me with a little more insight: college graduate, twenty-eight, single, a Virgo, and employed by the state in the customer support field. Her interests included computers, eating out, musical instruments, shopping, traveling, video games, writing, baseball, basketball, golf, fashion, film/movies, beauty/fashion, current events, health, and investing. She also enjoyed listening to Caribbean/Reggae, Hip Hop/Rap, Jazz/Blues, and R&B.

Although her profile stated she was single, I wanted to know how much that held true. With us having much in common, I decided to send a note.

Nice page. Nice pic, too. I'm sure your man wakes up with a smile every morning. I know I would…well, you would, too. (LOL) Hit a brotha up when you can.

NuSpot22

For about two weeks, I lived on the hope factor. I *hoped* she would respond. I *hoped* she liked my photo on my page. I *hoped* I didn't sound corny in my message to her.

But her reply ended my worries.

Thanks for the compliment. Unfortunately, I'm single and sleep alone. However, I do wake up with a smile on my face, but it has nothing to do with a man. By the way, I checked out your page. You don't look so bad yourself. I see you're a Sagittarius, thirty, and work in the field of technical support. I also see we have a lot of the same interests. So, NuSpot22, tell me what's not mentioned in your bio.

From that day on, we've been emailing each other nonstop. After several days of chatting, she divulged her real name, which is Diamond Sparks, and that she lives in New Brunswick, New Jersey.

Not too far from East Orange where I live, I wrote back.

In one email, I stated her username is misleading, and she replied by saying, *It's not misleading. It's MsDrippingWet.*

Just what I liked...a woman with a sense of humor.

We learned so much about one another and about our families. She's the middle of an older and younger brother, just as I am. However, we live in two different worlds. Mine requires a day to day survival technique, living in a concrete jungle; whereas hers is much more peaceful, much more colorful. In spite of our differences, we both have dreams and aspirations of being successful. We agreed that marriage came before children and a career came before them both.

Two weeks into our online relationship, I wrote, *If you ever would like to match the voice with the emails, you can hit a brotha up on the cell at 973-555-5555.*

Even after exchanging numbers, we seemed to chat more online than speak on the phone.

Diamond,

I understand we both have hectic work schedules, but we should make the time to meet. I would love to wine and dine you for an evening. What do you say?

NuSpot22

Diamond kept coming up with reasons why we couldn't meet, but after about four weeks, she finally gave in to my persistent nature.

We decided to meet for dinner at Frederick's Soul Food Café located in the downtown section of Newark. Having both eaten there once before, we agreed the food was superb enough for us to have our first date at the establishment.

So there I was sitting alone at a table in the far back of the dimly lit restaurant. I made reservations for 8:00 P.M., but Diamond was already fifteen minutes late and she hadn't even bothered to call. Twice the waiter had come over to see if I was ready to order. Each time, I would reply, "Five more minutes," and then continue sipping on my Sprite with lemon.

The restaurant was packed because of their "Martini Friday" special. The live DJ entertained the patrons by playing classic cuts from the sixties and seventies. Candles flickered on every table, providing a very intimate and trendy atmosphere. Mostly, I appreciated the smoke-free environment.

As the minutes passed, I couldn't help but to think she stood me up. What was I thinking? I hated blind dates. This reminded me of the time I met someone else online. We chatted for a couple of weeks and then decided to meet. We exchanged photos; hers was a headshot and a little blurred. I figured it was due to poor resolution.

We decided to meet on the corner of 8th Street and 6th Avenue, the village section of New York. Nervously, I awaited her arrival. Expecting to see someone on the scale of Janet Jackson, Halle Berry, or Beyonce, I was instead greeted by the complete opposite. My blind date turned out to be six feet tall, three hundred pounds, missing a front tooth, and reeked of serious body odor. Out of common courtesy, I tried to go through with the date, but when she started sharing her jailhouse stories, I made a quick exit and never looked back.

Now here I had possibly placed myself in another similar situation. My eyes kept searching the restaurant and over by the bar, hoping Diamond would show up. If she turned out to be a no-show, I promised myself to never date online again. After about twenty minutes of waiting, I decided to call it a night. Just as I pulled out my wallet to leave money for the soda and a generous tip for tying up the waiter's table, I noticed the host pointing in my direction. Standing next to her was Diamond Sparks, who looked even better in person.

As Diamond made her way over to me, I performed a mental checklist, comparing her appearance with how she had described herself to me over the net. Her hair was cut short. No way near as short as mine, but more like a classic Halle Berry style, giving emphasis on her perfectly round face.

Her caramel complexion will blend perfectly with my dark skin, I thought.

She indeed stood five feet six inches tall, just a few inches shorter than me, and weighed approximately one hundred and fifty pound, which she carried in all the right places. Her denim blue jeans hugged her like a second layer of skin. She left open her button-up brown sweater, revealing the white fitted tank top underneath. It was obvious she wasn't wearing a bra. With it being the end of summer, and the weather too unpredictable, I could definitely understand her reason for wearing a sweater. On her feet she wore brown, low heeled shoes. She accessorized with tastefully-placed jewelry, adding sparkle to her alluring style: a watch on her left wrist, diamond studded earrings, diamond necklace, and a diamond ring on her right index finger. In her hand, she carried a brown leather purse with a thin strap.

Yes, she was every bit of the woman she had described and the beauty her picture depicted. She caught the attention of many patrons—men and women. Some women had to check their dates for staring so hard. Suddenly, I found myself nervous.

We were the perfect couple online, but meeting face to face could change things for the worst.

Then, it came to my attention that we were practically wearing the same colors. I wore a dark brown, collared, button-up shirt, blue denim jeans, and light brown causal shoes from Aldo. I kept the jewelry simple, though, only wearing a sports watch on my left wrist.

Maybe this is a good sign, I thought.

Once Diamond reached the table, we embraced and then took our seats.

"You're much cuter in person," she said while placing her purse on the table.

"I'll take that as a compliment."

We both laughed.

"Yes, it is. I'm sorry I'm late. There was an accident on the parkway. I tried calling you, but I kept getting your voicemail."

"For real?" I looked down at my cell phone and noticed I didn't have a signal. "Sprint."

We laughed again.

The waiter approached and took our orders. Diamond

ordered smothered chicken, collard greens, and macaroni and cheese. She also asked for a glass of water with lemon and an apple martini. I ordered the same sides, but with honey glazed salmon. I didn't need any alcohol at the moment. I wanted to wait and see how the night unfolded.

Minutes later, the waiter returned with Diamond's drinks and stated that our food would be out shortly. During the wait, our conversation flowed, never missing a beat. The smiles on our faces indicated we were having a pretty good time. Her mental definitely matched her physical appearance…stimulating.

In the middle of our laughter, Diamond's cell phone chimed. She pulled it out of her purse and looked at the caller ID before answering. "Hey, girl…yeah…okay…I'll call you later." She hung up and placed the phone back inside her purse.

"Is everything okay?" I asked.

"Yeah, that was my girlfriend just checking up on me."

I'm sure the phone call was planned as a way to bail her out if things weren't going well.

Our meal finally arrived, putting our conversation on hold. We tried to speak between bites, but it was a losing battle.

The food was delicious. For dessert, I ordered banana pudding and she asked for the sweet potato pie. After that, we could barely move.

"It never had a chance," I said, referring to how fast I devoured everything on my plate.

Diamond smiled. "I put a hurtin' on it myself. I'd be big as a house if I did this everyday."

Women are always making references to their weight, no matter how good they look, I thought.

"Let's go work it off," I replied with a mischievous smile.

"Excuse me?"

"Let's go to Brokers."

Brokers is a famous night club in East Orange, a spacious establishment with two levels of entertainment. It's decorated with many mirrors and booths for people to be seated, and is fully air conditioned. Occasionally, there is a live performance on the upper level, but that wouldn't be the case tonight. More than anything, I just didn't want our date to end.

Diamond gave it some thought. "Okay, but I have to use the ladies' room first."

As she rose from the table and walked away, I couldn't help watching the nice view from behind. Only after she disappeared from my view did I flag down our waiter for the check.

"You ready?" I asked after she returned to the table.

"Sure." To my surprise, Diamond reached into her purse. "How much is the bill?"

I smiled at the gesture. "Tonight's on me. Your money is no good here."

"Thank you," Diamond said as I reached into my pocket and took out enough to cover our meals and the waiter's tip.

I believe a couple should compliment one another, and from the looks on many of the faces as we were leaving, we could've easily been voted Couple of the Year.

After leaving Frederick's Soul Food Café, Diamond followed me to Brokers.

It was still early, about 10:00 P.M. There wasn't much going on, so we decided to sit at the bar on the lower level.

"What are you drinking?" I asked.

"I'm not sure. What about you?"

"Long Island."

"Sounds good to me."

I ordered two Long Island Iced Teas. While sipping on our drinks, we managed to talk over the music. I, for one, am not a big conversationalist, so I let her do most of the talking. We talked about religion. Neither of us is a follower of religion, but we have a strong belief in God. We also discussed how life has changed drastically since President George Bush took office.

An hour later, and after I paid for two more Long Island Iced Teas, Diamond removed her sweater and held it in her right hand as we staggered onto the dance floor. The effects of the alcohol had definitely crept up on us, but we managed to move to the beat…or so we thought.

Wanting to find out how well Diamond could dance, I moved in closer, placing my hands on her waist, when the music went from a serious mix of Club to Reggae. We became so comfortable with each other that I moved even closer, brushing my chest against her breasts. Her sweet smelling perfume put me in a trance.

I didn't understand the lyrics, but the hard sound of the

drums took control of my body. I didn't care how silly or offbeat I looked. The spirits of the alcohol had infected our minds, and we became lost in the mood and the power of the dance.

As I pressed my body against hers, I'm sure she felt my manhood rising against her inner thigh. When she didn't pull away, this encouraged me to take our dirty dancing even further. I moved my left hand from her waist to the middle of her back and pulled her deeper into me. My right hand moved down to her apple bottom and cupped her ass.

By this time, a crowd started pouring in and we were dancing amongst many other partygoers. She was completely turned on and so was I, not caring who was watching. Many eyes were on us, but we carried on as if we were alone. We bumped, grinded, pumped, and gyrated our bodies into one another. We went down to the floor and back up again. I was determined to keep up.

She then turned around and gave me all she had back there. All I could do was hold on to her hips and enjoy the ride. My dick was literally trying to bust through my jeans. Diamond moved so sensuously that I could've sat in a chair watching her until I came. She was just that good, just that hot, and those hips swayed from every angle possible.

Women are good at doing that…moving like they're making love on the dance floor and acting as if they have no idea they are driving the man crazy.

"Damn, baby, I see your work. I can handle it," I managed to slur.

She turned around and looked at me with lazy eyes. "Can you? I don't think so."

I was definitely up for the challenge, not needing any help from security or anyone else in the club. That's why I couldn't understand why this guy came up dancing behind Diamond, pressing his body against hers. I wanted to attack him like a pit-bull, but to my surprise, she didn't seem to be offended by his gesture. Instead, she turned around to see who it was. He must have met her approval because she looked at me and smiled. As a matter of fact, she began dancing even harder, throwing her ass into him and pulling me into her as if to take us both on.

This stranger and I quickly became acquainted with eye contact. He smiled at me, but I didn't think this was a laughing matter. He was invading my space, and I felt the only way to get him to back off was to out dance him, show Diamond that I knew how to work her body.

Crouching down, I placed my head between Diamond's thighs, indicating I wasn't afraid to enter her dark valley. I pressed my face into her crotch, letting her know I could work the middle, and then slowly came up with my left leg between her legs. I positioned my erect dick so that it could fit perfectly between her thighs and pressed my body firmly against hers. We locked our bodies on Diamond's, sandwiching her, preventing her from moving freely.

"Work that shit, baby," the stranger commanded Diamond. "Come on, give it to me. Do it. Show me what you workin' with."

Diamond gave a seductive smile, closed her eyes, licked her lips, and started moving her body like a snake. This upset me because they carried on as if I wasn't even there. Right about then, I wanted to reach into my pants, pull out my anaconda, and show them both what *I* was working with.

My competitor and I began groping and pumping her,

harder and faster, faster and harder, both trying to outdo the other. We were working up a sweat, and I was at the point of no return. I couldn't hold back any longer. I looked over at my challenger, who was really into riding Diamond's ass, and saw a painful expression on his face. It was obvious we were both in the same state of mind.

My body tensed, and almost in unison, the stranger and I started jerking our bodies. We released our tension and came in our pants right there on the dance floor. From the smile on Diamond's face, I figured she knew what had just happened. My competitor lowered his head and staggered away in defeat.

When the DJ switched from Reggae to Hip Hop, Diamond and I took it as our cue to exit the dance floor. With it now close to 2:00 A.M., we decided to leave the club. As we walked to her car, she put her sweater back on.

"You sure you're going to be all right driving home?" I asked before she got in.

"I'll manage."

"You know, you can always stay over at my place."

Diamond smiled. "Sounds tempting, but maybe next

time."

"So there *will* be a next time?"

"We'll see."

"I can follow you home. Make sure you get there safely. Besides, I still would like to know why you call yourself MsDrippingWet."

Diamond contemplated for moment before stepping in closer to me. She unfastened the button to her jeans, and then in a single motion, she grabbed my hand and placed it in her pants. I rubbed the crotch of her soaked panties. After she pulled my hand back out, she fixed her clothes.

"Damn, baby," I replied, rubbing my fingers together until her fluids dissolved into my skin. "You know you dead wrong for that. You need to let me handle that for you."

She just continued smiling. "Like I said, sounds tempting, but maybe next time."

"Why put off until later what we can do now?" I asked in a pleading tone.

"You're cute."

Then she leaned in and we kissed. Our tongues met and

my hands immediately searched her body. I embraced Diamond and held on for dear life, not wanting to let go. After what seemed like an eternity, we pulled apart.

"Okay, NuSpot22, I'll give you a call."

Diamond got into her BMW and pulled out into the street while I watched her drive away until I could no longer see her taillights.

Good Neighbors

I stood in the doorway of Jasper Good's apartment looking at the damage the busted water pipe had caused.

"It's obvious you can't stay here," I said, thinking out loud, which is something I've been doing a lot lately. In my younger years, I was known for keeping a tight lid on my thoughts and an even tighter lid on my emotions.

"Where is he going to stay?" asked Pamela Justice, who stood next to me. At age twenty-five, Pamela had no problem sharing her thoughts. As a lawyer, she was even paid to do it.

Because Jasper stood there among the destruction looking so sad, I said the first thing that came to my mind. "You can stay with me."

Jasper looked at me strangely, but before he could object, I added, "It will only be for one night. The plumber told me everything would be okay if no water goes through those pipes. The water is turned off in this unit for the night, so we don't have to worry about any more flooding."

"I don't want to crowd your space," Jasper replied. Although he was well over six feet and a muscular young man, he looked like a little boy in his confusion.

"I have a three bedroom apartment," I reminded him. "You could lock yourself in one of those rooms and blast your rap music, or whatever you listen to, at full volume and I wouldn't hear a thing."

Jasper looked over at Pamela, as if he expected her to say something. It was like our lawyer friend had suddenly become mute, but there was no hiding the question in her big brown eyes.

"Well, it would only be for one night," Jasper said like he was convincing himself that the move was all right.

At that point, I seriously thought about withdrawing my generous offer and giving him money to check into a downtown hotel overnight. That was when Pamela found her voice and put her two cents in.

"Jasper, what about our project?" she reminded him.

The mention of the "project" snapped Jasper out of his daze. "Everything I need is right here," he said, "and if Amanda doesn't mind me working in one of her bedrooms, we should be all right."

I had no idea what project they were working on, but as long as it didn't involve hanging from my light fixtures, I couldn't see how it would be objectionable to me.

"Like I said, if you lock the door, you'll have all the privacy you need," I told them.

"Well, you know Jasper is working on a one-man show that is opening at the Imani Gallery next week," Pamela began, speaking like she was in a courtroom, "and he has to finish this last piece."

"Which involves you in some way?" I interrupted, getting a little tired of Pamela meddling into Jasper's affairs. This wasn't the first time she had done just that. Although they seemed to be the same age, I always got the impression she felt she had to protect him. Protect him from what I was never sure, but I knew she had a lot to say about how Japer conducted his dealings.

"Look, Jasper, I know you're tired of working on Wall Street and really want to get yourself out there as an artist," I said, speaking directly to the young man. "You've let me see some of your work, and I know it's just a matter of time before you make a name for yourself in the art world. If I can't help you, I won't hurt you, you can be sure of that."

"Well, it's just that the project involves me and…" Pamela hesitated to finish, and I detected some embarrassment on her part. I had no idea what that was about, but I wanted to get back to my apartment.

"Look, you can both spend the night in my apartment," I offered generously.

They looked at me like I had a head growing out of my shoulder.

"Look, I know Jasper likes to work late into the night." I paused to check my wristwatch. "It's ten o'clock now, about an hour from my bedtime. This old lady is about to turn in and should be in dreamland around twelve. All I ask is that in the morning when you two leave, you lock my front door behind you. Understand?"

They both nodded and looked sheepish, like I had caught them doing something naughty. Until then, I had no idea that they were fucking each other. Still, it was none of my business.

"Now, when you two leave in the morning and I find something missing, I know where to find you," I said jokingly in an attempt to lighten things up.

Jasper chuckled and Pamela brought forth a weak smile.

"Thank you, Amanda," he said to me. "And you're not an old lady."

"How old are you, Jasper?"

"Twenty-five."

"I'm fifty-six, and old enough to be your mother."

"You don't look like anyone's mother."

I smiled and nodded, graciously accepting the compliment. "Well, I workout every other day in my home gym, and I've been blessed with good genes."

"Fifty-six!" Pamela exclaimed, looking like she was in shock. "I would have guessed around forty, but no more than that."

"You young people are too kind." I didn't want to tell them my special diet consisted of having as much sex as possible. I didn't want to shock the little innocents, but I was still a sexually active woman, finding sex to be great exercise and an appetite suppressant. Why age when you can fuck? The only problem was that men my age couldn't keep up with me; they just didn't have the stamina. Because of that, most of them accused me of getting my kicks elsewhere. True, I enjoyed younger men, but not as young as Jasper Good.

Although, from time to time, I'd catch Jasper sneaking a peek at my long, lean body, fooling around with him would be like robbing the cradle. As far as he was concerned, the only thing old about me was the sprinkle of gray in my shoulder-length dreadlocks.

"Bring whatever art supplies you need over to my apartment," I instructed Jasper. "Pamela can give you a hand. I'll leave the door unlocked."

"I can't thank you enough for this, Amanda," Jasper said before I left the two of them alone to gather the material for their project.

My third and last husband was an artist, a painter like my young neighbor, so I knew it would take a little time for Jasper to get all of his equipment together, especially when he had to move it from one place to another. While I waited for him, I tuned into my favorite radio station, which played the best music from my era, the '60's, '70's, and '80's. Most of the time, I would turn the radio on and let the music flow through my apartment.

As I sat on my high-back, wrap around, earth-toned leather couch, Teena Marie soulfully sang "Behind the Groove." I was so absorbed in the music that the knock on the door startled me. Turning the music completely off, I rose to open the front door.

"I expected you to come right in. The door was unlocked." I was somewhat surprised to see Jasper standing by himself.

"I always knock," Jasper replied as he walked pass me carrying an easel and a black cloth over the canvas he was working on. He also carried a bulky black bag with a long, thick shoulder strap that I assumed contained his painting supplies.

"Follow me," I said as I led him through my living room and down the long, narrow corridor to one of my guest bedrooms.

"This is nice," Jasper said, looking around the sparsely furnished, but elegant bedroom. Inside, there was a queen-sized bed, a polished oak wood dresser, a comfy settee, and an antique standing lamp that flooded the room with a soft light. "Would it be all right if I moved things around a bit?"

I raised a skeptical eyebrow.

"Nothing major," Jasper assured me. "It's just that I like a lot of space when I paint."

"I can understand that. Move what you have to, just put everything back when you finish."

Jasper nodded. "Fair enough."

I watched him from the doorway as he set his canvas on the easel.

"You mind if I take a peek?" I asked, pointing toward the covered canvas.

He suddenly looked like a deer caught in the headlights of an oncoming car. "I'll have to talk it over with Pamela first."

"Pamela's the model?" I was really surprised because I had pegged the young lawyer as a stuffy tight ass.

"No comment," Jasper said, and then smiled broadly.

"Maybe there's hope for her after all," I thought out loud. I always loved the idea of sexually liberated women, but I knew becoming that woman wasn't an easy task.

"What do you mean, Amanda?"

"That is one beautiful girl who spends too much time hiding her body. I mean, look at those baggy business suits she always wears."

Jasper had to nod in agreement. "Getting her to pose was a major production," he admitted. "For two weeks, it was no, then maybe, then yes. That's why it's so important we finish this project tonight. I can't have Pamela back out on this."

"I would love to know how you got her to drop her panties," I said, probing gently. "To pose naked."

"I like to say nude."

"Nude, naked, whatever. You got Miss Prissy Pamela to expose her naked splendor. Was this before or after you slept with her?"

Jasper looked at me like I had slapped his mother. "What makes you think I've been sexually involved with Pamela?"

"I was married to an artist, Jasper. He fucked all his models before and after we were married."

"Did you ever pose for him?"

"Yes, but not in the nude. I drew the line there. I just couldn't adjust to the idea of thousands viewing my bare ass displayed in some art gallery. I still can't believe you got Pamela to expose herself like that."

"I didn't tell you she posed for me," Jasper responded, a bit too quickly.

"Your little secret is safe with me," I said while gently touching his face.

Jasper still had a look of distrust. "We can't discuss this in front of Pamela."

I drew an imaginary line across my lips, as if zippering them shut, but Jasper didn't look the least bit at ease. "Look, let me get back to the living room. Pamela might be trying to get into the apartment."

I left Jasper alone in the bedroom, which was now his art studio. When I entered the living room, there was a soft knock on my front door. Upon opening it, I found Pamela standing there in changed clothes. Now she looked like an African princess in her Kenté cloth caftan that flowed loosely from her neck to her ankles. On her feet were black flip-flops. It was obvious she was not dressed to impress. It was like she had no idea how sexy she could be with little effort.

"Thanks for opening up your place to us," Pamela said as she stepped inside. "Beautiful," my guest exclaimed as she took in the mixture of modern leather furniture, Afro-centric designs that included end tables carved from African tree trunks, and a fireplace adorned with floor to ceiling gold marble.

"Thank you, Pamela. Jasper is waiting for you down the hall," I told her.

But it seemed like Pamela didn't want to move. "Did Jasper tell you about our project?" she tentatively asked.

"Why? Do you want to tell me about it?"

Pamela actually blushed. "I'm doing it for my good friend Jasper, Amanda."

I really didn't know what to say. Was I supposed to commend her because she had made this great sacrifice? I felt that whatever I said would sound cynical, and I really didn't want to come across like that. I wanted to be supportive. It wasn't everyday a woman allowed a man to paint her naked, I mean in the nude.

"I remember the last conversation we had," Pamela reminded me, "you told me I should loosen up."

"What I said, Pamela, was that you're a beautiful girl and you don't do as much as you could to enhance your beauty…to bring it out."

"I'm not one to spend hours in the mirror."

"I can understand that. All I'm saying is you're a young woman. You should be enjoying your physical because it fades so quickly."

"So, in other words, I should flaunt it while I have it?"

"Something like that," I replied while walking over to my cherry wood and black leather built-in bar. "Would you like something to drink?"

Pamela surprised the hell out of me when she answered, "I'll have some white wine."

Not wanting to put pressure on her, I said, "I do have juice."

"I'd *really* like some white wine."

As she stepped up to sit on a high leather barstool, I poured some white wine for both of us. "A toast," I suggested

while raising my long-stemmed glass in the air. Pamela followed
my lead. "To great artistic creations and the significant role
models play."

Pamela nodded in agreement, and then sipped her wine.
I suspected the wine was to help her loosen up. My ex-husband
always supplied his models with reefer, what kids nowadays call
trees.

"You're here," Jasper called out as he joined us in the
living room. Noticing the look of distress upon his face, I offered
him some wine, but he declined.

"Is everything all right?" I inquired.

"Yes, but the lighting is better out here," Jasper informed
us, looking back and forth between me and his model. "Even
with the street lights coming through the window, the light is a
little too subdued in the bedroom."

"I have no problem with you setting up in here. Anything
for your art."

Pamela choked on her drink. "Isn't it a little, uh, open out
here?"

"We'll use the back bedroom," Jasper assured her. "We

can't just take over Amanda's apartment."

"Look, guys, it's getting late, pass this old lady's bedtime. I'm going to fill my glass with wine, and then retire to my bedroom so you two can work on your project. In here or in the bedroom, it really doesn't matter to me."

"Thank you for your graciousness, but I'm a little overexposed on this project," Pamela replied, obviously embarrassed, although she never did tell me how naked she would be.

"Pamela, I don't need to see you naked," I told her, thinking I was helping to get the show on the road.

"Did you tell Amanda I'd be naked?" Pamela asked Jasper, a look of hurt and betrayal on her face.

"I didn't talk to Amanda in any detail about the project," Jasper quickly said, while Pamela looked like she wanted to flee from my apartment.

"Don't make me regret agreeing to this, Jasper," Pamela snapped.

"Calm down, Pamela," I said, speaking like a Southside Chicago tough guy. "Jasper came in with a covered canvas, and it's still covered as far as I know. I haven't looked at it. He wouldn't let me. Help the man with his project, Pamela. Now, I'm going to bed."

The shocked look on Pamela's face almost made me laugh. With a big smile on my face, I walked down the corridor to the master bedroom.

While taking off my clothes, I couldn't stop thinking about Jasper and Pamela in my living room. Two healthy young black people and one of them naked. I kicked off my shoes and pulled my legs up onto my bed. Looking down at my bare feet and painted toenails, I wondered if I had missed something by not posing naked for my ex-husband. He had asked me many times, but every time, I thought about all the models he had painted and made love to, and I became insanely jealous. If truth be told, I also became self-conscious.

I had no doubt that Jasper's involvement with Pamela was strictly business, but Pamela was an attractive young woman naked before him, and that had to mean something.

I found myself getting off my queen size bed and walking over to my full-length mirror. Although the room was dimly lit, recessed lights bathed the front of the mirror and made me feel like a model in a picture frame. An attractive black woman stared back at me. Standing five feet two inches, I was one hundred and thirty pounds with 38D breasts and a tight waist. Sure, Pamela was much taller, leaner, and younger. Still, I was a woman that men looked at lustfully.

I stripped naked and stood in front of the mirror, trying hard to be objective about my fifty-six-year-old brown body. My nipples protruded like dark berries and my navel was deep. Although a little thicker than I liked, my waist tapered invitingly into my womanly rounded hips, and my legs were thick and sturdy. Many men lusted after me and I liked the attention. I wondered if I ever modeled for Jasper would he just see me as a "project" and not as a fuckable woman.

Casually, I found myself gently stroking my cunt. I had to admit there were many nights lately that I couldn't sleep unless I stroked my clitty and made my love come down in a gush of juice that coated my fingers. Not wanting the night to be another solo sex session, I brought my hands up to my belly, and then I turned to get a clear side view of my body, especially my ass. It was firm, but not as high as it used to be. Still, I had no doubt a man would like to smack it, lick it, and suck between the cheeks where it was sweet, or at least that was what I had been told by various lovers.

Inspired by the sight of my ripeness, I reached behind and grabbed my ass with both hands, squeezing it like I imagined a lover would. Each of my three husbands loved my ass, and all of them loved to fuck it. I allowed this, but not all the time, just on special occasions like their birthdays, anniversaries, or when our lust rose to a feverish pitch and spiraled out of control, making me want to give up my tightest hole.

In my bedroom, I found myself moaning as I bent at the waist, my hands still filled with the full softness of my ass cheeks. I couldn't help but wonder how Jasper would feel in my ass…his big, young dick driving into me and pumping me hard as I urged him to slap my ass hard. It wasn't long before I was bent over even further while stroking my clitty with a free hand. I stopped myself just short of an orgasm, but there was no denying the wetness that had collected in my cunt.

With a deep sigh, I climbed under the sheet on my bed. Not long after dozing off, I was awakened by laughter coming from the living room. Then there was a soft knock.

"Yes," I called out while sitting up in the bed and pulling the sheet around my body.

"It's Jasper, Amanda."

"Come in," I said as I pulled the sheet tighter around my torso.

Jasper came in smiling, naked from the waist up.

"Who's painting who?" I wondered out loud as he stood in the doorway.

The young man actually blushed. "I just like to be comfortable when I work."

I understood because my ex liked to work in his boxer shorts, saying it was his way of making his models feel comfortable. *Real comfortable before he fucked them,* I thought bitterly.

"You all right?" Jasper asked. "I only knocked because I was coming from the bathroom and saw your door slightly open. I hope we weren't too loud in there."

"Are you finished?"

"No, just taking a break."

"I dozed off, but not into a deep sleep."

"I was wondering if you wanted to see the painting."

"Did Pamela leave?"

"No, she's still here. We talked, and she said it seemed silly not to let you see the painting, especially when you opened your home to us."

"I'd love to see it," I told him. "Give me a few minutes to put on a robe."

"Great." Jasper smiled, and then closed the door.

Getting out of the bed naked, I went into my walk-in closet and pulled down a cream-colored silk robe. Checking myself in the mirror, I pulled my hair off my shoulders and into a ponytail. When I entered the living room, I found Jasper with his shirt back on, but unbuttoned, and Pamela sitting on a barstool with a glass of wine in her hand.

"How's the model?" I asked Pamela.

"I've never been so relaxed," she replied, her long Kenté cloth caftan billowing around her like a parachute.

I knew I was a stark contrast to her in a robe that hugged my every curve like a lover, and wondered if Jasper noticed. If he did, he was gentleman enough not to stare and played it real cool. I looked over at him, disappointed that he had decided to cover his manly torso.

The canvas cloth was off the painting. It was Pamela, and she was naked…nude. The back shot prominently exposed her back, a side view of one breast, and all of her full, firm, young ass. She exuded seductiveness and innocence. She looked like a young woman that did not know her true beauty, and therefore, could not be accused of flaunting it. However, she had a lot to flaunt, especially that ass, two perfectly formed globes separated by a deep crevice.

I looked over at Pamela and thought she would blush when she realized I had taken in the full glory of her nudity. No blushing from Pamela this time. As a matter of fact, she stared me down. For some reason, that shook me; it was like she was challenging me, forcing me to show my feminine side. I walked over to the bar to make myself a real drink. A gin and tonic is what I needed.

"Would anybody like a mixed drink?" I asked out of politeness more than anything else; I didn't see Jasper or Pamela as serious drinkers.

"A gin and tonic for me," Jasper said as he proudly looked at his painting.

"Anything for you, Pamela?"

"I'm okay with the wine," she replied, relaxing on the barstool like she had no place to go and all the time in the world to get there.

"I thank the two of you for sharing the painting with me," I said while walking over to Jasper to hand him his drink.

"I'm surprised you never posed for an artist," Pamela said as I turned away from Jasper.

"It's still not too late," I said jokingly. "It's obvious Jasper likes painting naked women. I am a woman, and I can get naked."

Jasper laughed out loud when he saw the shocked expression on Pamela's face.

"You'd get naked, just like that?" Pamela asked, her big brown eyes widening.

"What is nudity but another form of self-expression," I said flippantly.

"Would you get naked for Jasper?" she asked, as if daring me to cross a certain line.

"If he asked nicely," I replied, my eyes now on Jasper.

"You'd make an excellent model," Jasper let me know, using the glass in his hand to indicate that me as a model was of some interest to him.

Overly conscious of the eyes upon me, I walked back to the bar. I drank my drink a little faster than I should have and found myself choking. Jasper came to my rescue, patting me hard on the back. As he spoke to me, he allowed his hand to linger on my back.

"Pamela can't believe a woman can be totally comfortable in the nude."

Suddenly it dawned on me that Jasper saw me as some kind of liberated woman. I didn't see myself as that, but I liked to have a man, a special man, enjoy the sexy curves and smooth softness of my body.

"We all came into this world naked," I responded, not really sure where I was going with my pronouncement. It seemed like the hip thing to say, and because I was the center of these young people's attention, I didn't want to come across as un-hip.

"Have you ever been to a nude beach," Pamela asked.

"Yes, with my first husband. He was Brazilian."

"Were you self-conscious that first time?"

"I was too high on reefer to care, Pamela. I was also drinking Tequila shots, so any inhibitions I had were left at the hotel we vacationed at."

"I didn't know you were that open-minded, Amanda."

"Not so open-minded. Just young and carefree. I was your age then, equipped with what I thought was a great body."

"That's why you say I should be freer? To share this great body with whoever wants to see it? To flaunt it?"

"Not flaunt it, Pamela. I never said flaunt it. I said enjoy it. Enjoy the firmness, the sweetness, the juiciness."

"It's real juicy," Pamela commented, "but not too many men know or appreciate that."

I looked over at Jasper, who turned away, looking sheepish like he felt the need to apologize for Pamela's openness. That was when I got the feeling something had gone down between them. That Pamela wanted something to happen, and for whatever reason, it didn't.

Pamela rose and stood on unsteady legs, and I got the impression the wine had gone to her head. "Not every man can appreciate a juicy woman. Have you always been a juicy woman, Amanda?"

"I'm still a juicy woman," I told her, letting her know she wasn't going to get a rise out of Jasper by attacking me or putting me down. No way would I let her push me into the shadows just because she was a much younger woman.

"That's what you say, but what do the men say?" Pamela stated the question so harshly that I took it as a personal challenge.

"I believe men still find me juicy," I said, hoping to bring an end to our going back and forth in front of Jasper.

"Do you find Amanda juicy?" Pamela had to ask Jasper.

I waited for him to reply and felt like a prisoner waiting for the guillotine. With Jasper being so respectful of my age, I felt he didn't see me as a sexy woman, because to do so would be disrespectful. However, he surprised me by walking over and standing beside me, making me feel so small and vulnerable before him.

"I find Amanda very juicy," he said as he stroked my shoulders.

"Which part of her body do you find the juiciest?" Pamela wanted to know, determined to push it to the limit and beyond. "Her tits or her ass?"

I felt Pamela had taken everything too far, but there was no turning back for Jasper; he couldn't help but feel like he was being challenged. We all knew he had to prove to Pamela how juicy he found me. Holding onto my thin shoulders, he lowered his lips to my mouth. I closed my eyes as his lips touched mine and his tongue dueled with my tongue. There was a lot of juice generated with that deep soulful kiss.

"That was juicy," Jasper said as he pulled back from me and wiped his mouth. The one kiss made me want more of him.

"Wow!" Pamela exclaimed, her sarcasm in full effect. "Where else is Amanda juicy?"

Without saying a word, Jasper pulled open my robe and fondled my bare breasts. I moaned and pushed my nipples into his hands. I even arched my back so his fingers could tweak my nipples. The top of my robe fell to my waist and was held in place by my tightly belted sash.

"Oh, baby," I groaned as he sucked on my nipples. He also rubbed my bare back, making me even hotter. I prayed he would continue to find me juicy, because I really wanted to feel his hands all over my body. When I knew I couldn't take any more, I sat him down on the barstool and opened his shirt.

"Why don't you take it off?" Pamela called out to me. "I know Jasper won't mind being half-naked, especially since we all came into this world naked anyway."

I didn't appreciate Pamela's sarcasm, but I was determined to show her that I was the belle of the ball, the ebony diva at this party. In one swift motion, I pulled Jasper's shirt completely off his torso. When he was bare before me, I rubbed his manly chest and tweaked his nipples. Because I allowed myself no restraint, I covered his nipples with my teeth, tongue, and lips while standing between his legs and rubbing up against the bulge of his hard dick.

"You need to let me show you a thing or two," I said as I looked over my shoulder at Pamela who was still standing by the bar.

"Go for it," Pamela replied. "I can't even get a rise out of Jasper. I guess I'm not juicy enough."

"Instead of feeling sorry for yourself, Pamela," I snapped, "you need to take matters into your own hands." While speaking those words, I proceeded to rub my hands up and down the crotch of Jasper's pants.

"You don't have to prove anything to Pamela. I think she's just buzzed from all the wine she drank."

That was when I unbuckled Jasper's thick belt, unbuttoned his pants, and pulled down his zipper. Then, I reached into his pants to free his big, juicy dick. It was a beauty, not only big, but thick and long. I held it so Pamela could see it. My mouth watered at how delicious it looked.

"Now this is juicy," I exclaimed while stroking it. I didn't stop until I saw pre-cum collect at the tip. "I know you know what to do with something like this," I said to her.

Pamela walked over to Jasper like she was hypnotized. "He wouldn't let me see it. He wouldn't let me touch it."

"That's all you want to do?" I asked and stepped back

when she moved to grab Jasper's dick. "Just see it and touch it?"

Pamela closed her eyes as she stroked the dick that was standing at attention. "I want to taste it," she admitted. Her body shuddered at the thought of taking Jasper into her mouth.

Standing beside Jasper, I lowered his pants and boxers. Then he stepped out of the puddle of his clothes and moaned loudly as Pamela stroked him, up and down, slow and steady.

"Taste him," I invited Pamela. "Put him in your mouth."

On her knees now, Pamela took Jasper in her wide mouth. She couldn't deep throat him, but she did get a lot of his dick inside her mouth.

"Suck it, suck it good," I encouraged. While Pamela sucked Jasper, I tickled his balls and rubbed his ass. She proved to have a real juicy mouth as she slobbered and hummed on his manhood.

"You want some?" Pamela asked me when she finally came up for air. "Do you want to suck his dick?"

I nodded as I gave one final squeeze to his ass. Moving in front of him, I got on my knees, then licked the length of his dick before taking him in my hot, wet mouth. I didn't stop licking and sucking until he shuddered, yelled out, and came in my mouth.

"You swallowed it," Pamela said as if I had accomplished some impossible task.

"When you love a man," I told her as I wiped my lips, "you have to love all of him."

Then I led Jasper by his dick to the master bedroom, with Pamela following closely behind. Once inside the bedroom, I untied my sash and let my robe fall to the carpeted floor.

"You shaved it all off," Pamela said while staring at my crotch.

"It's juicy, too," I replied, stroking my throbbing cunt as Jasper lay naked across my bed. I climbed up his long body until my cunt was positioned over his mouth. Not needing any instructions, his long tongue emerged from between his lips and licked me until I released into his mouth. Suddenly, I felt drained. Jasper had hit the jackpot when it came to my body.

After climbing off Jasper, I found Pamela standing near my mirror. "Now is a good time to discover how juicy you are," I said as I walked over to where she stood.

"What are you going to do to me?" Pamela asked with

fear in her eyes.

"Nothing you don't want me to do," I assured her. "But we've got to get rid of this."

With us working together, Pamela's cloth covering came off over her head. Beneath it, she was naked. From where Jasper lay on the bed, he had an excellent view of our bare asses. As I stood behind Pamela, I gently stroked her high, young bottom. It was full, firm, and juicy. She moaned loudly as I played in the humid and wet crack of her smooth ass cheeks.

Suddenly, Jasper appeared in the mirror, standing behind us. He, too, rubbed on Pamela's luscious bare bottom.

"Hold her ass open," I told Jasper, "while I get on my knees and bury my face in her ass."

That was what I did until sweet Pamela shivered and climaxed with a deep shudder and a loud moan. She came so hard that she became weak in the knees and Jasper had to carry her to my bed. After laying her down, she reached up to wrap her long arms around his neck. She pulled his head down to her and jammed her tongue into his mouth. They started rolling around on my bed, with Pamela ending up on top.

"I want to see you ride his dick," Pamela told me as she slid off Jasper's chest.

I watched lustfully as she lay beside Jasper and grabbed his dick. But her mission wasn't to just stroke him. She placed herself so that she was across his torso, her head near his groin. Then I watched as Pamela held the dick with her hand and bathed it with her tongue. Jasper moaned, groaned, and squirmed, but Pamela wouldn't let him go.

"Now," she said as his dick pointed straight up to his navel.

I moved forward to straddle Jasper's thick, hard thighs. I rubbed against his hard-on, wetting his dick with the juices flowing from my cunt. Grabbing Jasper's dick, Pamela placed it at the entrance of my cunt. I then leaned forward and she pushed his dick inside me. I screamed because it felt so good inside me, filling me so damn good. After placing both of my hands onto his chest, I rode his sweet dick like there was no tomorrow. Pamela boldly playing with my ass enhanced my fucking. I screamed again when she stuck a finger into my wet asshole. As I humped Jasper, she moved her finger in and out of me.

"Fuck...Me!" I yelled as I creamed all over Jasper's steady pumping dick.

After cumming hard like that, I pushed Pamela onto her back. I kissed her hard in her mouth, and became overly excited because she greedily accepted me. I didn't know how I could've ever seen her as a prissy tight ass. In my bed, she proved herself to be a wild woman. Her hot body was non-stop movement as I licked and sucked her breasts, belly, and hairy, but neatly trimmed, cunt. She was so wet that her juices glistened like pearls in her pubic patch. Her clit peeked out from the mound of black hair as I nibbled on her sweet, young cunt. She came loudly and her body jerked out of control.

"I never fucked Pamela," Jasper told me as he sat up in my bed, his eyes filled with lust.

"Do your thing, young man," I suggested as I stroked his dick and then led him into Pamela.

In a post-orgasmic stupor, Pamela threw her legs wide open for Jasper. He eased into her and made her tremble, his dick pushing into her hot cunt. "Good dick...good dick," she chanted as he threw his slim hips into her. "I knew it would be some good dick. And big, too."

I watched in amazement as Jasper took over Pamela's cunt, banging her so good that her womanly juices overflowed and ran down the crack of her bouncing ass. Not to be left out, I fondled Pamela's breasts and rubbed her clit as Jasper fucked her. When she came, she wrapped her arms and legs around him tightly. I placed my hand under her hot bottom as she convulsed around Jasper's big, juicy dick.

We made love that night and all the next day, stopping only to drink, eat, and nap. We got together a few times after that, but it was never as good as the first time.

Mending a Broken Heart

It was another night of fighting. For weeks, Tara Moore had been trying to convince her husband to come clean about his affairs, but he would always throw his hands up in frustration and make it seem like she was the problem. She had let their three children stay over her girlfriend's house so they could get to the bottom of their problem once and for all.

"Just tell me the truth," she pleaded as tears welled up in her eyes.

"You don't want the truth. You'll just start crying." He paused, and then as if having a change of heart, he said, "You know what…I'll tell you the truth. The truth is we haven't had sex in weeks. You're talking about *I* changed? *You* changed," he said, pointing an incriminating finger. "You don't do half the things you used to do."

"What are you talking about? I do everything!"

"It's still not enough! Tara, let's stop playing games. Let's not fool each other anymore. This marriage has been over for a long time." Then, he walked out of the bedroom as if nothing more needed to be said.

Whoever said words will never hurt you must have never loved. Tara wanted to charge after her husband and physically release all of her anger and frustration, but she couldn't move. She just stood speechless as if the wind had been knocked out of her. She tried to catch her breath, but needed to get out and get some air. She desperately needed someone to talk to, someone she trusted enough to confide in. The only person she could always count on for words of encouragement and guidance was her mother, who was deceased, and speaking to spirits sometimes wasn't enough.

Her insides were enflamed and her mind in a daze. Her world had just came tumbling down. Her husband had become insensitive, a mere stranger to her now.

Without thinking, she reached into her pocket and pulled out the business card of a male friend of hers, Tobias Fox, who she ran into earlier that day while at Hue-Man Bookstore on 125th Street and Frederick Douglas Boulevard. They hadn't seen or heard from each other in over a year. He happened to be there conducting a book signing for his latest novel, *Mending A Broken Heart*. They had met two years ago, back when she was happy, at a previous job and became friends. He had moved from Newark, New Jersey, and now lived on the upper eastside of Manhattan not too far from where she lived in Harlem. He always said one day he would become a bestselling author, and now he was living out his dream while she was living a nightmare.

"Hello," Tobias answered on the second ring, his soothing voice comforting. She tried to speak, but her emotions got the best of her. "Who is this?" he asked.

"I'm sorry to call you like this, but I didn't have anyone else to call."

"Tara?" he asked, looking at the Caller ID.

"Yes," she replied while sobbing and trying to pull herself together.

"What happened?"

"It's my husband. We had it out."

"Did he put his hands on you?"

"No, but I can't stay here with him anymore."

"You can come to my place. You need me to come get you?"

"No, I'll catch a cab. Are you sure it's okay?"

"Yeah, you don't need to be there tonight." After giving Tara his address, he said, "Call me as soon as you get in the cab."

After hanging up the phone, Tara grabbed her purse off the end table and headed toward the front door of the two-bedroom apartment. As she entered the living room, her presence startled her husband. He tried to discreetly hang up his cell phone, but she was too familiar with his sneaky behavior and at this point didn't really care. They said nothing to each other as she passed him and left.

He redialed the number on his cell phone, and on the first ring, she picked up. "I'm sorry about that, babe. The signal dropped. I don't think you should be alone tonight. I'm about to come over."

"I'd like that," she whispered in a soft, seductive tone.

"Okay, I'll see you in a few." After ending the call, he went to the bathroom to freshen up for his mistress.

Once she hit the damp street, Tara managed to flag down

a cab. The light rain made this gloomy fall night more depressing. Once inside, she told the cabdriver her destination and then called Tobias, who informed her that he would be standing outside of his building waiting. During the ride, she couldn't help but to think about her marriage and how it had fallen apart.

Two months after they met, she became pregnant with her second child. Four months later, they were married. And now, four and a half years later with three boys, they were headed for a divorce. She didn't realize how fast time had flown by. If only she could ease down on the brakes a little to slow her life down.

Maybe we are better off as friends, she thought. That would probably be best, especially for their children. She was in a similar situation when twenty years old. Her mother had just passed from cancer at age forty-one; her father was MIA, lost somewhere in New York; and Tara's boyfriend at the time was not very supportive. She had no one but her two-year-old son. That was ten years ago, but it still felt like yesterday.

She knew raising three boys at ages two, four, and twelve would be difficult. Much of her worries came from fears: fear of having to do it all by herself; fear of dying young like her mother.

"Mommy, I need you. I'm scared," she whispered.

Speaking to spirits became a daily routine in her attempt to avoid flooding her mind with negative thinking, which would only make matters worst. Not wanting to be an emotional wreck when she met Tobias, she took a few deep, steady breaths to calm herself. Wiping the tears from her eyes, she noticed the cabdriver staring through his rearview mirror. To avoid eye contact, she looked out the window. She managed to smile upon reminiscing back to when she first met Tobias.

He introduced himself, and she asked, "Like Tobias from the HBO series, *Oz?*"

"No. Like Tobias from the Bible."

She thought his comeback was cute. After finding out he was a Sagittarius, she liked him even more. She wasn't deep into astrology, but she did believe the zodiac signs had meaning and purpose. According to Tara, Sagittarius was the best sign on the zodiac chart, besides Cancer, of course. Her mother was a Sag, and so were her grandparents. All were beautiful people, inside and out.

And so is Tobias, she thought.

Although looking forward to seeing him, she wished
it was on better terms. After leaving the company where they
worked, he had gotten heavy into his writing. They continued to
stay in touch, calling every so often, sending an email here and
there. But then she got pregnant with her third child and all of
Tobias' late night writing sessions finally paid off, landing him a
publishing deal. Eventually, they lost contact.

Maybe she should have married a Sagittarian, maybe not.
Two of her previous relationships were Sagittarians, but they had
serious problems. One was lazy, didn't want to work, and was
never there when she needed him. The other only wanted to work
if she was in his life, like she was his only reason for keeping a
steady job. His lack of motivation turned her off. Not to mention,
he had a temper and would try to get physical with her during
heated discussions.

She released a deep sigh. She was tired...tired of being the
husband and wife, the mother and father, the man and woman in
her relationships. Being so caught up in her thoughts, the sound
of the cabdriver's voice startled her.

"Mami," he said for the third time, "ten dollars."

She had reached her destination and didn't even realize it. Time continued to pass her by. While digging into her purse for money to pay the fare, Tobias approached, the doorman holding an umbrella above his head.

Tobias opened the back door. "Come on. I'll take care of this." Tara stepped out as Tobias handed the cabdriver fifteen dollars. "Keep the change."

"Thank you, Papi."

As the cab pulled out into the busy traffic, the doorman walked Tobias and Tara to the doorway of the building, shielding them from the rain with his umbrella, then held the door open as they stepped inside and proceeded to the elevator.

Tobias lived on the twelfth floor in a cozy one-bedroom apartment. The furniture, though sparse, was very tasteful and carefully selected. Paintings by Quaada were displayed on the white walls, and the polished hardwood floors were clean enough to eat off of.

Tara took a seat on the brown leather sofa in the living room, rubbing her arms as if she had suddenly gotten a chill. She felt a little uneasy running to another man for comfort. *But this is different,* she tried to convince herself. *Tobias is a friend.*

Tobias walked into the living room carrying a cup of hot tea and a napkin.

It's been nearly two years and he hasn't aged a bit, she thought.

She loved his dark skin and admired how he always kept his low afro neatly trimmed. His attire was sporty, an Adidas tracksuit and Adidas tennis shoes. As he sat down next to Tara, he handed her the napkin and placed the cup of tea on a small coaster that rested on the wooden coffee table.

"I made you some green tea with honey. It'll help you relax."

"Thanks. I see you're doing pretty well for yourself."

Tobias looked around his apartment, then back at Tara. "I'm doing okay. Just as long as I keep writing stories people want to read, I'll be fine. Where are the children?"

Tara tried to smile at Tobias' genuine concern. "They're staying over my girlfriend's house."

"So what happened?"

Tara released a deep sigh as if reliving the day's events

would be painful. "I don't even know where to start. Things
haven't been going too well." She tried to hide her sorrow behind
a smirk, but found herself fighting a losing battle. She used
the napkin in her hand as a shield when looking Tobias in the
face. She fought back tears as she found her voice. "He wants a
divorce."

"I'm sorry. Did you guys try counseling?"

"Please, he doesn't feel we need counseling. Besides, a
counselor can't make him love me," Tara replied, looking directly
at Tobias. "We haven't had sex in weeks. Today was the first time
we've actually spoken to each other in three days."

"Maybe you guys need to separate for awhile. Sometimes
the distance helps bring people back together, or at least
appreciate what they have. What's your husband's name again?"

"Jackass."

He laughed. She smiled. *This is a good sign,* Tobias
thought. Maybe it was best they didn't mention her husband's
name.

"My thing is…if he isn't there for me now, I don't want
to go through something drastic and have to worry about his

foolishness. He needs to go be with his other women and leave me alone. I want to enjoy life to the fullest without all the drama. There are so many things I haven't done yet, like go on a cruise. I've never even been on a plane. Bottom line, I haven't really lived."

"I hear you. You definitely shouldn't wait for your husband to get his act together to enjoy life. Nor can you force or make him be the man that you need or want him to be. Some things have to be taught, and apparently, no one has taught him how to be a husband or a responsible man."

"Yeah, I blame his upbringing for that. Every time he gets in a jam someone bails him out, so he doesn't know what it is to struggle. Unlike him, I've been through it all. From the death of my mother, who was really the only person I had looking out for me, to being homeless, I've been through a lot."

"And all of that has prepared you for this. You'll pull through."

"I guess. I'm just scared. My mother died from cancer at forty-one, my grandmother died from cancer at forty-four, and three of her sisters died from it, also. My doctor, who tested me last month, said I don't have cancer, but she found something else which may require minor surgery. I haven't told my husband about this, though."

"Why not? I think you should tell him."

"He likes to run his mouth to his mother and brother. Once they get a hold of information, everyone in the town knows it. People have always said his brother was interested in me. When I first met his family, his brother and uncle were always in my face. Their wives used to have fits, and they even started rumors about me as a result of their jealousy."

Tobias admired Tara's rich dark skin and long black hair. His eyes held onto her full lips as she proceeded to speak. "If I told my husband, his brother would have exaggerated the situation just to spite his brother, so I just ignored them all. His brother has even admitted on prior occasions that he is jealous of my husband."

"Wow. That's deep."

Tobias remembered how happy Tara was just two years ago. He always thought her to be the most attractive of all the women in the office, but once he found out she was married, he knew she was off limits. He had met her husband once, but not formally, when he came to pick her up from work one day. If only he could put a name with the face, her husband would be that much more real to him. They were carrying on as if Tara's husband was fiction, a character with no name. However, some things you just can't make up. Her story was very much real.

Tobias looked at the tea on the table. It was getting cold.

"How do you know he's seeing other women?"

"I'm not stupid. His behavior tells it all. I don't understand why men get married if they know they aren't ready to commit?"

"Men aren't as attached to their bodies as women are. We can have sex with a woman, and after it's over, act like nothing ever happened. We can spend the rest of our life with a woman, but to have sex with just one woman for the rest of our life," Tobias shook his head, "now that's a challenge. It's just not in our nature. That's a man's biggest fear when it comes to commitment."

"Not all men cheat," Tara said in defense of mankind.

Tobias smiled. "A man is as limited as his options. An

attractive man that has a little money, a car, his own place, and a decent wardrobe has way more options than a man who doesn't have these things. Just look at all the celebrities, high political officials, big-time drug dealers, and even dudes that make a decent salary. Women are throwing themselves at these people constantly.

"A friend of mine has been married for twenty years. He told me that if he was on an island and a beautiful woman approached him, and they had a mutual understanding that after sex they would go their separate ways, he would cheat on his wife. Until a man becomes truly focused on what he wants in life, he will always play the game. Most men fuck up when they try to carry on more than one relationship."

Tara couldn't believe what she was hearing. "I'd rather be single."

"All I'm saying is that a woman shouldn't leave a man for cheating unless it's excessive and he no longer loves her, because she's just going to leave the situation and jump into a similar one."

"If this is supposed to make me feel better, it isn't

working."

Tobias smiled; Tara didn't. The tea was now cold.

"I'm sorry," he said with a straight face.

"It's okay. Thanks for keeping it real with me. I just don't have the strength for this," she replied as tears began to burn the back of her eyes. "I can't even remember the last time my husband told me he loved me. I just want to be happy. I just want to have someone who loves me unconditionally, no strings attached. I'm getting up there in age, and I keep thinking about how my mother died at forty-one. I don't want to die."

As the tears fell from her eyes, Tobias moved in closer and pulled Tara into him. He wrapped his arms around her as if protecting her from the cruelty of the world. She welcomed his warm embrace.

"Stop," he said. "Don't talk like that. You're not going to die anytime soon. You have too much work to do."

Tobias tried to say the things he felt Tara wanted to hear, and Tara wanted to believe everything Tobias said. Sexually frustrated and emotionally drained, she was grateful for the comfort he was giving her, and for the warmth her body received from being pressed up against his.

Tobias tilted his head to look at her. Tara lifted hers to look at him. Their lips met. She pulled away.

"I've never cheated on my husband."

"I'm...I'm sorry."

"Don't be."

As they stared into each other's eyes, Tara realized she needed something stronger than green tea. She needed to feel loved. Tobias wanted to meet her needs. They kissed again, but this time with more passion. He sucked on her bottom lip. She sucked on his. Their tongues met and searched each other's mouths. It was sweet.

With no need to rush, Tobias wanted to take his time and ease some of her pain. He kissed every part of her face: lips, chin, cheeks, eyelids, forehead, and earlobes. He pressed his cheek against hers, smearing her tears on his face. When he pressed his tongue deep into the right side of her neck, her head fell back, she closed her eyes, and then exhaled. He did the same to the left side.

Taking her by the hand, Tobias pulled Tara up from the

couch and led her into his bedroom, where they undressed in the dark. Her breasts were full, hips wide. Even in the darkness, she felt insecure about her body and tried to cover up. Tobias smiled, thinking her shyness was cute. He then walked closer and moved her arms to her sides.

"It's okay," he said, taking a step back so he could get a better look. "You're gorgeous."

Tara couldn't tell if he was lying or not, especially since she never thought of herself as being attractive. During her childhood, she was picked on because of her dark complexion. Her mother said she was beautiful. Her husband said she was fat. Now a person she hardly knew was admiring her body.

But he isn't a stranger, she thought. *His name is Tobias Fox and we're friends, and friends help friends in times of need. Right?*

"Wait, Tobias. This isn't right," she whispered.

But Tobias wasn't listening.

She battled with her conscience, knowing their actions were wrong, but her hormones overpowered any form of righteousness. She was trembling. He sensed her fear and they kissed, which helped her relax some.

Tara wrapped her hand around his long, hard dick and became weak in the knees. It had been a long time. She placed it between her thighs, closed her legs together, and locked onto it. Backing up, they used the wall for support. She was tired of feeling alone. She needed the comfort of a man. They began grinding, and she pressed the length of his dick against her clitoris.

As they kissed, Tobias cupped her right breast and gave it some special attention. He rolled his tongue over her nipple, sucked on it, and then did the same to the other. Next, he pressed both breasts together and sucked on both nipples at the same time. Having her breast sucked and clitoris stimulated simultaneously almost caused her to climax.

Pulling away, he got down on one knee and kissed her inner thighs.

Tobias looked up to Tara as if he was about to propose. "Show me," he commanded.

She spread her lips, revealing her clit. It glistened. Tobias reached behind and grabbed Tara's soft, round ass. She squatted some and he pulled her into his mouth. She obviously enjoyed the pleasure of having her clitoris sucked and pulled on. She released deep moans and groans, speaking a language only she could understand. She didn't want to cum this way, but the more she tried to pull away, the more he pulled her into him. She didn't want to fight; she had no more energy to fight, whether in the mental or physical sense.

Giving in, and with her back pressed up against the wall, she managed to place her right leg over his shoulder and grab onto his hair. Tara's body tensed up. She wanted to escape the tight grip of his lips and run for the door, but she was no longer in control. Tobias had her pinned, refusing to release her until she released all of the frustration built up inside of her. Gyrating her body, she threw her hips into his face, while pulling him by the hair into her.

Just before she came, Tobias backed off and Tara nearly fell to the floor, but she managed to use the wall to help balance her and slid straight up. Tobias stood to an upright position, grabbed her by the hand, and led her to the bed.

"Lay on your side."

Tara followed his instructions, lying on her left side. She

didn't want to talk. Talking would only bring on guilt, and guilt would bring on regret. And right now, she didn't want to feel either. She watched as Tobias walked over to his dresser, pulled out a Lifestyle condom from a top drawer, and rolled it on. He then lay behind her on his side, lifted her leg, and slid inside.

As Tobias took his time going in and out of Tara, she used her left hand to rub her clit and her right to squeeze her nipple, doubling the pleasure. He then lifted her leg up higher and managed to maneuver himself on top of her without sliding out. He rested his body on top of hers, staring into her watery eyes. They kissed.

Her mind was pleading with him not to stop as he explored her inner walls. Their breathing became heavy; her emotions were building; his climax was rising. Her body tensed, and she dug her nails in his back. He screamed out in pain, but didn't stop. It just made him move faster, harder.

She made a public announcement. "I'm about to cum! I'm…about…to…"

She came, releasing a flood of emotions as tears fell from her eyes. He followed her lead and came as well. They embraced, or more like held on to one another, with their chests heaving while trying to regain control of their exhausted bodies.

Tobias pulled out and rolled over onto his back. He wondered what would become of their relationship now. Tara turned on her side, placing an arm across Tobias' chest.

Two wrongs don't make a right, but it sure felt good, she thought before drifting off into a deep sleep.

Porn Star

It was the summer of 1999 in Cali when my older brother LaMonte came to me with his wild ass scheme. He told me what he had in mind and I wasn't impressed at all.

"Tony, you saw the video last night," LaMonte reminded me.

I nodded, remembering the fat white guy with eyeglasses and long brown hair. He was in a cheap hotel room with a beautiful young white woman who was there to have sex with him on camera.

"His name is Ed Powers," LaMonte went on. "His *Dirty Debutante* series has been going on like forever."

"I don't see how he does it," I admitted in wonder and envy. "He's no stud, not even handsome."

"Yeah, but you saw the scenes he put together with those three fine looking females."

"Maybe he drugged them," I suggested, trying to make a

joke. LaMonte wasn't having it as we walked and talked along the boardwalk at Venice Beach. He was serious as a heart attack.

"They all seemed pretty eager to me," LaMonte said, and then ran a hand over the lower part of his bearded face. Ever since we were children, he had always played around with the camera.

"All right, I can see where you're coming from," I reluctantly admitted. "You can leave this Ed Powers in the dust. You're handsome and a real stud. So what are you going to call your video series?"

"The *One Hundred Percent Video Virgin* series."

I smiled at my brother. "That's hot. Now with that Ed Powers, it was obvious he had more than one cameraperson. Who are you gonna work with?"

"You," LaMonte answered with a straight face.

I laughed because I couldn't take a decent picture to save my life. Now a video camera I know is different, but still, I knew I wouldn't feel comfortable being my brother's cameraperson while he got down with a fine honey on the bed like Ed Powers. I thought maybe I could even recruit some of the talent. There were many beauties on Venice Beach, and I always thought I had a pretty good feel for those who were young, single, and eager to mingle. In other words, ready to give up the ill nana.

Because of my minor celebrity status as a semi-professional footballer, I had my share of hot and heavy one-night stands. I also felt that if ordinary looking Ed Powers could pull some fine honeys, then my brother LaMonte, who was slim, handsome, and looking like Teddy Pendergrass with his dark beard, could have his pick of the litter. Still, I didn't see myself as a cameraperson. Turns out, neither did LaMonte.

"You'll be the on-camera male talent," LaMonte informed me, and once again, he wore no smile upon his face.

I tried to laugh. "You see me as Ed Powers?"

"I see you as Sean Michaels or Mr. Marcus," he replied, naming two black porno stars that were handsome, muscular studs. They performed with a rainbow of women of all colors and races, and both of these black men directed and produced their own videos. Michaels owned his own company, Sean Michaels Productions International, and his sister Sandi worked with him. Still, I was a little uncomfortable with my brother pimping me as a porn star.

Ironically, our first production was not a young, hot-bodied Venice Beach honey. I guess this is a good time to set the record straight. Most folks think *California Love* with Jesse, real name Cassie Lawrence, was the first Beach House production. It was an early video release, right before *Flippin' On A Dirty Mattress,* the video that put Beach House Productions on the map. As a result, we won the Best Ethnic Video at the AVN awards show. That unexpected honor put us up there alongside adult video companies like Vivid Video, Anabolic, Video Team, Heat Wave, Elegant Angel, Jake Steed Productions, Sean Michaels Productions, and West Coast Productions.

One day at Venice Beach, while out "scouting for talent", we met our first video virgin. The night before, we had decided on a criterion for our Beach House honeys. We didn't want any porno veterans. We also didn't want any silicone-enhanced honeys, natural breasts only. Even if their tits sagged a little and there were some stretch marks on their asses, it was okay, as long as it was natural. That's what we wanted, what we were looking for.

We decided LaMonte would do the interviews with the talent off-camera and I would take care of the on-camera sex scenes. Also, onscreen, I wanted to be known as Mandingo Man.

"Like Superman?" LaMonte asked as we walked along the boardwalk.

"More like Super Black Man."

"Oh, so like an alter ego?"

"Yeah, more like that. I'm gonna have to do a little acting to get through this, LaMonte. I'm not an exhibitionist. I mean, I like to get down, but to have someone watching and filming me…well, that's gonna take some deep concentration."

"The way I'll shoot it, you won't know I'm there."

"Trust, I'll know you're there, brother." *And the honeys will know, too,* I thought as we walked and talked. There were a lot of slim bodies whizzing past us in tiny tops and skimpy bottoms on roller blades, but LaMonte didn't seem to be impressed by any of that.

"Black, White, Hispanic, Asian, it doesn't make any difference to me," I let my brother know. Because he was deep into his talent hunt, he couldn't respond to me. "And she doesn't have to look like a *FoxTrapper* centerfold," I added, *FoxTrapper* being our favorite skin magazine. This was long before we met *FoxTrapper* publisher Miles Monroe and he invited us to develop a series of videos in conjunction with his magazine.

During the summer of 1999, Beach House Productions wasn't a blimp on the adult video scene. We were nothing but aspiring video production entrepreneurs with wild dreams of becoming millionaires…no scratch that, billionaires.

"There she is!" LaMonte shouted as he stood looking over a railing and down onto the beach.

The woman he pointed out to me was the most unlikely choice for a porno flick. She had the body, long and tall in platform sandals, wore short denim shorts with a navy blue bikini top, and had mocha skin. She carried a blanket and was looking for someplace to sun herself.

"See her?" LaMonte asked, obviously excited.

"I see her, but you can't be thinking about using her as a video virgin."

"Why not, Tony? She's hot."

"Yeah, but, LaMonte, she's no spring chicken. Look close. She looks old enough to be our mother, or even our grandmother. I'll admit that she's well preserved, but…"

"Grannies need love, too."

"Don't play with me, LaMonte."

"Baby brother, listen to me. It will be a novelty, something totally unexpected."

"I thought we were doing video virgins, not video grandmothers."

"Man, she might not even go for it, but if we could get her to sign a release, we'll bring a whole new thing to the marketplace."

"I hear you."

"She's hot, LaMonte."

"So it's a go?"

"Let's do the damn thing."

" 'Cause if we can pull this off, we can start Beach House

Productions with a bang…me banging and her whimpering.

"We laughed together, and watched the grown and sexy woman as she sat upon her red blanket. Out of a big straw bag, she removed oversized sunglasses and a bottle of sunscreen. Her body glistened in the sun as she applied the protection. LaMonte looked at her so intensely that she caught his eye and waved, probably thinking she knew him from somewhere.

Speaking of recognition, I am always amazed by the number of people that have recognized me in either *California Love* or *Flippin' On A Dirty Mattress.* I consider myself an underground performer, far from the mainstream, but folks from all walks of life have seen these videos and, whether it is rental or straight out purchase, they have made it possible for me and my brother to drive top-of-the-line SUVs and never have to worry about money. But, I'll tell anybody, my best performance was my first time in front of LaMonte's camera, inspired by a woman who convinced me that "age ain't nothing but a number."

When we finally started toward her, she was picking up her stuff and walking off the beach. We had to walk fast to catch up to her. Still, we didn't want to come at her like breathless idiots. We almost lost her when she went into a little magazine shop. I ran, leaving my brother behind because I wanted to see her up close. I was intrigued because even looking in her face, it was hard to tell her age.

The magazine shop was small, but had three aisles. After entering the shop, I panicked because I couldn't find her. Like a madman, I frantically searched each aisle, began to sweat, and then turned a corner and literally ran right into her. I slammed into her and she dropped the magazine she had decided to buy.

"Excuse me," I said as I bent to pick up the magazine. On the floor between us was the latest issue of *FoxTrapper*. "This yours?"

She blushed and reached for the magazine. "Yes. Thank you." She grabbed the magazine and took it to the counter. Fumbling into her big straw bag, she got her money out.

"Wait!" I called as she hurried out of the shop.

She stopped to allow me to catch up with her. There was a mischievous twinkle in her light-colored eyes.

"Wait, please."

"Haven't you embarrassed me enough?"

I smiled at her, turning on the charm. "That was never my intention."

"You're probably wondering why I would buy a men's magazine, right?"

I figured it would be best for me to say nothing, to let her talk.

"I read the articles. I find them fascinating. When I was growing up, people didn't speak so frankly about sex."

"I didn't stop you to talk about *FoxTrapper,* but I must admit I enjoy the magazine myself. I just can't remember reading any of the articles."

She laughed, and then covered her mouth. "So why did you stop me?"

"To get to know you."

"With all these pretty young things around here? You want to get to know me?"

"Age ain't nothing but a number."

"That's what I always tell myself when I get into my daughter's clothes."

"Those are your daughter's clothes?"

"Everything but the platform shoes."

"It all looks good on you."

"Thank you, young man. You are so good for my ego. I feel a little less self-conscious now."

"You have no reason to feel self-conscious. You're a good looking woman."

"I should make you stop, but I'm enjoying all this attention from a handsome young man so much."

"You're in great shape. How do you do it?"

"I swim. I also do calisthenics, yoga, stretches, watch what I eat, and travel as much as I can afford. Keeps my mind open."

"I like a woman with an open mind."

"I bet you do," she replied, and with that one statement, I knew she had game and might be open to a Video Virgin experience. Still, I couldn't rush her. I looked around for

LaMonte, but he was nowhere to be found.

"Who is she?"

I turned back to her when she asked that question.

"I'm referring to the girl you're looking for. You seem a little distracted."

"I was hanging out with my brother, and now, I can't find him."

"When he looked at me…stared at me really…on the beach, I thought I knew him. That's why I waved at you two. When he turned away, I knew I was wrong and was embarrassed."

"He should not have been staring."

"Actually, I was flattered. A young, handsome man looking at me like that does wonders for my ego."

"You're not used to men looking at you?"

"Not me, maybe at my three daughters."

"You have three daughters?" I asked, surprised. With her slim, tight body, I figured her to be in her late forties, but not with three daughters, unless she began her family while very young.

"I'm here in California because my youngest, at age twenty-four, just got hitched."

If her youngest is twenty-four, I thought, *then...*

"I'm fifty-six."

"You look good! Damn good!"

She actually blushed. "Thank you."

"I mean it. When did your daughter get married?"

"Yesterday. I decided to stay over an extra night at the Venice Beach Hilton. Her new husband paid for my suite. I tried to talk her out of marrying him, though."

"Why?"

"I see her following in the footsteps of her sisters. Married and locked down, saddled with too many babies, too soon. No future goals for herself. I have six grandchildren. All my girls married young. I wanted them to travel, to see the world before they settled down, get to really know themselves. They were all too scared to do that. They all wanted security."

"Where is your husband?"

"He's dead."

"I'm sorry."

"It's been twenty years. I, too, married young."

"And there's been nobody else for you?"

"You ask a lot of questions, young man."

"Sorry."

"A lot of personal questions."

"I'm interested."

"In me?"

"Yes."

"You don't even know my name."

"What *is* your name?"

"Hillary Boston."

"I'm Tony," I told her, and we shook hands like we were sealing a deal. That's when I heard the click of LaMonte's camera.

"I had to do that," LaMonte told us. "You two make a hot

couple."

"You must be thinking about *How Stella Got Her Groove Back*," Hillary said, then laughed.

I introduced her to LaMonte, and then we walked along the boardwalk, getting to know each other.

"I live in Florida," Hillary added as we all sat in the dining room of the Venice Beach Hilton. She invited us to have lunch with her, saying, "It's not everyday I get the complete attention of two handsome young men."

Hillary ate a fruit salad, while LaMonte and I put a hurting on some burgers and fries.

"You two can have that because it's obvious you young men work out. I wish I had that kind of discipline, to build me some nice big muscles."

After a few more bites of her salad, she asked what we were doing on the beach. Without any hesitation, LaMonte told her, and to our surprise, Hillary wasn't shocked or disturbed. Like she said, she had an open mind. Then, LaMonte told her what he wanted to do with her.

"Aren't I a little long in the tooth for that?" Hillary asked. "LaMonte, what young man would get all hot and bothered by seeing me in a video?"

I smiled because it was a lot easier than I thought it would be. Not that Hillary said yes right away, but she was obviously intrigued enough to consider our proposition.

"You're a fine looking woman," LaMonte told Hillary, "and sexy as hell!"

Hillary Boston self-consciously touched her short, dyed blond hair, which was a nice compliment to her tanned skin. She looked from me to LaMonte, and then said, "I just don't know if me with my legs up in the air would be a pretty sight. I could never see myself like that in a picture, and you're talking about a video. How could I do that?"

"Just relax and you'll be great," LaMonte assured her, talking like he had videotaped many women just like her. His confidence was infectious; I felt there was no way Hillary Boston from Florida could say no.

That was when LaMonte excused himself to get his video

camera equipment out his SUV. When he returned, we followed Hillary up to her suite.

"Make yourself comfortable," Hillary said when we walked into her hotel suite. The centerpiece of the room was the big double bed with clothes strewn all over it. "As you can see, I wasn't expecting any company."

I went over to the floor-to-ceiling window as LaMonte rearranged some of the furniture.

"I wore this for the wedding," Hillary said, holding up an elegant black gown.

"Put that on," LaMonte suggested.

Hillary looked surprised that he would such suggest such a traditional outfit. "It's sexy, but not that revealing. I thought you wanted a real hot video?"

"I do, but I want you naked beneath the dress."

Hillary giggled. "That would be real naughty, huh? I'll be back in a sec."

LaMonte looked over at me as Hillary disappeared into

the bathroom. "You ready, little brother?"

"I'm Mandingo Man," I let him know.

LaMonte smiled, and then said, "I got that memo. You're ready. She's ready. It's gonna be hot, off the chain, ridiculous up in here!"

When Hillary emerged from the bathroom, LaMonte had his camera on his shoulder with the additional lights shining on her.

"It's so bright in here," Hillary commented.

"The more light, the clearer the picture," LaMonte explained.

"You like?" Hillary asked as she posed near the bathroom door. She wore a black halter tuxedo gown with a wrap front and satin lapels. Her smooth long back was bare and inviting; I found myself wanting to run my tongue all up and down it.

"I don't believe I'm doing this," Hillary said as LaMonte zoomed in on her.

"You'll be fine," LaMonte told her.

"I don't think I can take you both."

"I'll be busy with the camera," LaMonte let her know. "My brother will have the pleasure of making love to you."

Hillary giggled. "I truly hope it is a pleasure. I'm not very experienced. I've only had two men in my life: my husband and a man I tried real hard to fall in love with after my husband passed. He was so nice to me, but I just couldn't marry him because I didn't love him like that," she rambled. "I'm a little nervous. My palms are sweating."

"We'll take it nice and slow," LaMonte assured her.

"Nice and slow," Hillary echoed.

I stood where Hillary could see me, and see how much I really wanted her.

"You looking at me like that," Hillary told me, "makes me melt."

"I want you," I said while rubbing the outline of my hard-on through my pants.

"It's been a long time for this old woman," Hillary said as

I took her in my arms. I bent my head to kiss her wet and hungry mouth. Before I knew it, her hands were all over me; she even grabbed my butt, pressing her body hard against me.

"It's gonna be so good," I whispered into her ear.

"This is the good thing," Hillary said as she rubbed my hardness through the front of my pants. "Please, don't hurt me with that good, big thing."

With her hands on me, all I could do was moan loudly.

With long delicate hands, Hillary unzipped my white linen pants and pulled them open. "Can I suck it? Can I take it in my mouth?"

That was when I pushed my pants down and stepped out of them. Using both her hands on my dick, Hillary pulled me over to the bed. As I pulled off my white linen v-neck top, she sat on the edge of the bed.

"You're all naked," Hillary observed as I stepped to her. She moaned deeply as she licked up and down the length of my rock hardness. Then, she licked my balls and rolled them around in her wide mouth. In the porno industry, we called this "tea bagging".

As Hillary sucked and moaned, she gently squeezed my butt. Suddenly, she sat back on the bed. "I'm a little embarrassed," she admitted while wiping her lips. "I've never attacked a man like that. It's been so long. I, uh, I guess I'm a little hungry."

Naked, I stood by the bed. Extending my hand to her, I pulled her up beside me.

"What you do to me, what you do to me," Hillary exclaimed as I turned her around and pressed my hard-on into the slickness of her gown-covered bottom. "You make me want to be a wild woman."

"I like wild women," I replied while nuzzling her neck. Hillary squirmed in my arms as I held her around her waist. "We got all night," I added as I opened the gown. She held her arms up as I pulled the gown down to her waist. With her naked body pressed against my naked body, I pushed down on the gown until it was a puddle of material at her feet. I rubbed my hands up and down the sides of her body as she stepped out of her gown.

"Oh, yes," Hillary moaned as I fondled her large breasts,

squeezing the dark nipples between my fingers. "You make me crazy, crazy!"

"Let's get crazy together," I suggested as I gently pushed her onto the bed.

On all fours, facing away from me, Hillary's bottom was full, round, and shiny with sweat as she poked it out at me. To make her real crazy, I opened her cheeks and licked down to her pussy. She grunted, trembled, and came.

"Oh…no," Hillary said breathlessly as she lay flat upon the bed. "I'm so embarrassed. I didn't mean to cum…that fast. I didn't even get you inside me."

"It's okay," LaMonte said from across the room.

"Is that the way you wanted it?" Hillary asked, pulling her naked self together and sitting up.

LaMonte came in for a close up of Hillary looking dazed.

"Did you want me to cum first? Is it over? I want more. I'll probably be sore tomorrow, but I want more."

"You want him inside you?" LaMonte asked, still working

his camera.

That was when Hillary decided to get modest, pulling the sheet up to cover her naked torso. "I want him inside me. Yes."

"In your pussy?" LaMonte asked.

"Yes."

As Hillary looked up at LaMonte, I pulled on the edge of the sheet.

"I've never had anything that big inside me," Hillary let us know.

"Inside your pussy?" LaMonte said, moving all around Hillary who followed him with her eyes.

"Yes," Hillary replied with much force as the sheet slipped off her body. She sat with her legs slightly spread and her hand on her round thighs. "In my wet pussy," she said as she looked down at herself.

"Show me your wet pussy," LaMonte gently directed.

Hillary leaned back a little as she opened herself for the prying eyes of the camera. She moaned as she rubbed her clit, and then stuck a finger inside herself.

I joined her on the bed, running my hands along her smooth shoulders.

"I still want you inside me," Hillary informed me. "I want to cum with you inside me."

It was an Ed Powers moment when Hillary reached out to grab my dick. As she squeezed it, I rubbed her breasts and palmed her butt.

"Call him Mandingo Man," LaMonte told Hillary as she bent her head to suck me.

"Mandingo Man, Mandingo Man," Hillary chanted between sucks and licks. She made me grunt when she took most of me into her wide, wet mouth. "I want dick," she wasn't ashamed to tell me.

I slid beneath Hillary, and she let her big round butt sink into my lap. She grunted when my hard-on went right up into her guts. With her in the reverse cowgirl position, I pumped it into her nice and slow. She rode up and down on my lap like she was on a trampoline, letting my dick probe the sugar walls of her middle-aged pussy.

When we were downstairs, LaMonte explained to Hillary Boston how our little scene would end.

"Why like that?" Hillary wanted to know, never having seen a porno tape.

"It's the money shot," LaMonte patiently explained to her.

Hillary held herself like she was chilled. "It would be so much better if Tony came inside me, flooding my insides with his cum."

"No one would be able to see that, Hillary."

"But it would be so good inside me. A woman longs for that. I even came when my husband squirted in me like that."

"The audience has to see that, Hillary. They have to know that Tony came."

"I don't like it."

"I know, but it's the money shot."

In the suite, I dug deeply into Hillary, pumping into her as she lay in the missionary position, which she loved. She stroked my butt as I did my thing, her eyes closed as she moaned loudly beneath me, her body hot and wet. She threw it up at me, her heels behind my legs.

I hated to do it, but I had to announce, "It's time," because the way Hillary was socking it to me, I couldn't hold out any longer.

After our porn star reluctantly took her legs from around my lower back, I moved her into the doggy position and rode her ass like that. Then I placed her on her back and knelt on the bed, my dick in my hand. As I jerked off, Hillary reached up to tickle my balls. I grunted as my load shot out onto her heaving chest. But even after I came, she wasn't finished with me. While kneeling on the bed beside me, Hillary sucked the head of my dick and stroked the length of it. She even called me Mandingo Man without LaMonte telling her to.

It wasn't long before we said our goodbyes and went our separate ways, congratulating ourselves on a job well done. Unfortunately, you'll never see *Mandingo Man with the Greedy Granny* because Hillary Boston from Florida never signed a release.

Spanish Fly

It turned out to be a night I'd never forget. We planned to meet
straight after work at the China Club in midtown Manhattan.
Sofia and I hadn't seen each other in weeks. The last time we
spoke, she was crying so loud on the phone I couldn't make out
a word she was saying. It took her nearly twenty minutes to calm
down. She and her boyfriend, Angel Martinez, had just broken
up for the third time.

Apparently, she found out about another female he was
dealing with. Why she kept getting back with that deadbeat was
something I never understood. It's like some women are magnets
to heartache and pain.

We'd met two years ago while working at a law firm.
Two weeks after she was hired, I noticed her sitting alone during
lunch. It was the perfect opportunity. I could've kept going about
my business, but she was too damn fine to look the other way.
She carried herself in a conservative manner, wearing a dark blue

pantsuit with dark blue heels. The only jewelry she wore was a set of diamond studded earrings, a Gucci watch, and a Louis Vuitton handbag that sat in a nearby chair. Her fair, but nicely tanned complexion set well with her natural brown curly hair, soft inviting brown eyes, and full luscious lips.

I have to admit I was a little intimidated, but managed to build up enough courage to say, "I don't mean to intrude, but is this seat taken?" It was lame, but it was all I could think of at the time.

She smiled anyway and said, "Oh, no, not at all." Her Spanish accent almost put me in a trance. I'm sure she was trying her best to be nice. When I asked her name, she said very proudly, "Sofia De la Cruz-Gonzalez."

It was a strong, but interesting name that seemed to have meaning and purpose, unlike mine, Michael Moore.

During our brief conversation, I learned that she lived in the Bronx, was raised Catholic, is the oldest of three sisters, and is the first generation living in the states. Her parents were proud Puerto Ricans who refused to give up their native ways. They hardly spoke English or watched American television.

I wanted to learn everything there was to know about Ms. De la Cruz, but more importantly, I wanted to know if she was into dating black American men. I personally felt it was a bit immature to think that interracial dating was an issue, especially in this day and age, but unfortunately, not everyone felt the same way.

She wore no wedding band and stood five-five with a body that would put the Latina singer Shakira to shame, possibly no children. Although I wanted to, I decided against asking for her number. I had to remain cool, calm, and collected; didn't want to come off as aggressive or too eager. I had to wait for the right moment, and this first time encounter wasn't that time.

I then took the liberty of schooling Sofia on the ins and outs of the firm, who to stay away from and who to trust. We laughed, enjoying each other's company. She then excused herself and stepped away from the table. I couldn't help but stare at her hips swaying from side to side as she left the cafeteria. She was all that I ever dreamed of.

As weeks went by, I would make it my business to appear in the same places as Sofia around the firm, and always took lunch the same time as she. She sat a few cubicles away, and I managed to find reasons to stop by. I know it sounds obsessive, but I was on a mission to get close and personal with Ms. De la Cruz, my Latina princess.

Then that dreadful day came during lunch while eating and laughing it up with Sofia. Her cell phone went off. She reached into her handbag, looked at the caller ID, and then answered the call.

"Hola," she said into the phone. Her body then became tense. "Que?" she asked in an irritable tone. She then began speaking in Spanish, but switching to English from time to time. It was obvious she didn't want me to fully understand her conversation. Within minutes, she tossed the phone back into her bag.

"I'm so sorry about that," she said, trying to pull herself together.

"It's okay. Is everything all right?"

"It will be. My boyfriend gets on my freakin' nerves. He acts like a three-year-old sometimes."

I couldn't resist. I had to inquire about my competitor.

She told me they had been together for nearly two years. His line of work was in entertainment, managing artists, and it was interfering with their relationship. They met at Jimmy's in the Bronx. It seemed like what started out as a good thing had become a bittersweet fling.

I wanted to dig deeper, find out why she was still dealing with this so-called *Angel,* but didn't want to press the issue. I knew it was best to listen, play the role of a concerned friend for now. The thing with women having male friends is that most of the time the man patiently waits, no matter how long, for that storm to arrive. He catches her when she's most vulnerable, and then moves in, striking like lightening. Somewhere down the line, Angel would slip up and send Sofia running into the arms of another man for comfort.

Thanks to Angel, Sofia and I became good friends. I became her listening ear and shoulder to lean on whenever she was feeling down. I even bought a *Spanish for Dummies* CD set from Barnes & Nobles and learned how to prepare a few Spanish meals, like sweet fried plantains, arroz con pollo guisado *(rice and stew chicken),* pernil *(roast pork),* pasteles rellenos de papa *(stuffed potato balls)*, and sancocho *(stew)*.

I knew I was tripping when I started listening to the FM Spanish station and took a few salsa lessons. But I wanted to be more than prepared for if or when the opportunity ever arose. I wanted to get Sofia's parents' approval, let them know that I not only respect their culture, but their daughter, as well.

I always imagined Angel as some short, skinny geek with no class, who did not have the slightest clue on how to treat a woman, especially Sofia. That was until the day I saw him.

He came to pick Sofia up one day from work. He stepped out of the driver's seat, walked around, and leaned up against the car talking on his cell phone, wearing dark sunglasses. As I carefully studied my competition through the lobby glass window, I put me and Angel in a mental lineup to decide who would be the better man. He drove a Lexus, and I took the C train to Brooklyn. We both stood at five-eight. His curly black hair was cut in a low fade; mine was cut low, but tapered at the sides. His face was completely shaved, but I wore a shadowed goatee. He wore an iced out chain around his neck with a medallion I couldn't quite make out, an iced out bracelet on one wrist, and an iced out watch on the other with a couple of iced out rings on both fingers. The only jewelry I owned was a Guess sports watch I bought two years ago. It was obvious he was doing quite well for himself.

Angel was casually dressed on this mild summer day with a white fitted short sleeve t-shirt that showed off his muscular frame; I hardly ever worked out and could stand to lose a few inches around the midsection. There was a huge tattoo painted on his left bicep; I didn't see any point in permanently damaging my skin like that. He also wore blue straight-leg designer jeans and a pair of white running sneakers. I was dressed in a blue button-up collar shirt, brown causal slacks, and brown rubber sole shoes.

We were the complete opposite, but *I* being the one Sofia shared her deepest feelings with gave me the upper hand. It must be frustrating for a woman when she can't freely express herself with her man because of fear of him taking it the wrong way and blowing it out of proportion. I was tempted to pull out my cell phone and call the police. He probably had warrants or didn't have a valid license.

The sooner Angel's out of the picture, the sooner I'd have Sofia all to myself, I thought.

But as I began dialing 9-1—I heard someone call out my name. It was Sofia. I quickly ended the call.

"Hasta mañana, Michael," she said, waving goodbye.

"See you tomorrow, Sofia," I replied, smiling as I waved back.

As she approached, Angel greeted Sofia with a kiss on the cheek, and then opened the passenger side door for her. He had a little class after all. Then he got into the driver's seat and sped off.

Just be patient, my inner voice advised as I walked out of the office building and onto the street. *He'll slip up. Men always do.*

After about six months with the firm, Sofia announced that she was resigning. She managed to land a bigger and better opportunity with a large finance company that could use her skills in their legal department. Because the company was located in the city, we managed to meet up for lunch from time to time. I was still there for her in times of need. She said, "No matter what you will always be my friend," and I said, "No matter what I will always be here for you."

But that was then and this is now. Now I was planning to leave work for the day to meet up with my Latina princess. She called the night before, asking if we could get together for a few drinks. She wanted to celebrate for finally getting up enough strength to leave Angel for good. She also wanted to thank me for putting up with the late night phone calls and hour long lunches spent listening to all her sob stories.

Before leaving, I sprayed down with Obsession cologne. I wore black rubber sole shoes from Kenneth Cole, a pair of charcoal, casual straight-leg slacks, and a light grey button-up short sleeve shirt. I stepped into the men's room to give myself a final look over before moving into the next chapter of my life.

Talk about perfect timing. Just as I approached the China Club, Sofia pulled up in a cab. When she stepped out, it was all eyes on her. She demanded the attention of all those standing outside.

She wore a black, cotton, strapless summer dress that fell just below her knee, with a black satin sash tied around her waist. On her feet were black strap sandals with a heel. Her hair was pulled back and held together by a big black hairclip. Her diamond studs glistened and her Gucci watch made time stand still. If looks could kill, she'd be on trial for murdering the entire borough. She was definitely keeping it grown and sexy.

Ignoring the stares and whispers, Sofia walked up to me and planted a wet kiss on my cheek. Her sweet fragrance filled my nostrils, and I immediately became aroused. There was a crowd developing, but she informed me that we were placed on the guest list and able to go to the front of the line. I smiled, feeling like I had something every man wanted but couldn't have, and every woman desired to be, but didn't have what it took.

Inside the club, the DJ was playing a mix of current R&B. Because there was a small crowd, we decided to sit at the bar and order some drinks. I ordered a Bacardi and Coke with lime; she ordered an Apple Martini. It was hard trying to talk over the music, but we tried anyway.

"Thanks for coming out," she shouted with a serious expression.

"Thanks for inviting me," I shouted back. We smiled. "So

you finally left Rico Suave alone?"

"That's right," she said with a big, bright smile that could've lit up the dark room we were in. But then her smile faded to a look of sadness, and the room suddenly became gloomy. "I got tired of all the lying and different women. And we couldn't go anywhere without him making a scene. He is so freakin' jealous. It was driving me crazy. I mean, if a guy even glanced my way, he would make a big thing out of it."

"How did Angel take y'all break up?"

"Please, he begged and pleaded for me to give him another chance, but enough is enough. Now he can deal with whomever he wants to."

"Well, here's to your independence and liberation," I said, lifting my glass to hers.

"Free at last! Free at last! Thank God almighty, I'm free at last!"

We both broke out into uncontrollable laughter because she was really trying to imitate Dr. Martin Luther King, Jr., but wasn't even coming close.

By eight o'clock, a nice crowd had formed on the dance

floor. Sofia and I managed to guzzle down two drinks, and were filling a little tipsy. The DJ switched from Hip Hop to a serious mix of Reggaeton.

"Come on," Sofia demanded, pulling me by the arm. "Let's dance."

She didn't have to ask twice. We stepped away from the bar and made our way onto the dance floor.

We moved our bodies to the hard bass. I couldn't keep my eyes off my dance partner. Within seconds, she twirled her body around and backed that thing up on me. My soldier immediately stood at attention. I placed my hands on her shoulders and gently squeezed her soft skin. I closed my eyes, taking in this special moment, and pleaded with God that if I was dreaming to let me sleep until this dream was complete.

Sofia then threw her hands up in the air and wiggled her ass against my erection. I slid my hands down from her shoulders to her sides, grabbed hold of her shapely hips, and held on for dear life. Our bodies were now in sync.

My hormones were racing from all the excitement. I backed up off Sofia to put some space between us, not wanting to lose control and make a mess in my pants. On cue, she turned to face me and worked her hips like a belly dancer. The power of her movements almost knocked me offbeat. I was relieved when the DJ switched to Merengue.

Sofia noticed me leaving the dance floor and tried to convince me to take a few lessons. I was embarrassed enough. She held her hand out, but because I refused to accept her offer, a smooth Don Juan stepped in on my behalf. I didn't even trip, and neither did she.

The intruder began dancing with my partner. He moved like a native, giving Sofia all the spins and turns she wanted. He even made her laugh out loud as I faded into the crowd and became a spectator, clapping and urging them on.

She had moves like Jennifer Lopez, but with an attitude of her own. Together, they looked like they were doing an exaggerated *Hustle,* a classic seventies dance, but with a lot of fancy footwork and upper body movement. All I could do was watch in amazement.

The next song played must not have been liked by the partygoers, because they scattered from the dance floor like roaches when the lights come on. Sofia kissed her partner on the cheek and thanked him for the dance. He responded like a gentleman by kissing her on the hand and saying in a thick Spanish accent, "The pleasure was all mine."

"I see your work. You were definitely doing your thing," I said as she approached me.

She just smiled. "Come on, silly. Let's get another drink."

It was just a little after eleven-thirty when we left the China Club, and I wanted to get my princess home before twelve. She stated that she would be okay catching the subway, but I insisted on paying for her cab and riding along to make sure she made it home safe and sound. She was flattered, but tried to talk me out of it. I wouldn't budge, and to prove my point, I immediately sat in the backseat. After seeing that I was serious and had no plans of moving, Sofia got in and gave the cabdriver her address.

"You're crazy," she said playfully.

"I've heard that once or twice," I replied, smiling.

"Coño, my feet are killing me," she said, throwing her head back and releasing a deep sigh.

"Come here, let me see. I give a pretty good foot massage."

"Oh, really?" Without protest, Sofia loosened the straps to her sandals, stepped out of them, then leaned to the side and placed her legs on my lap.

I rubbed my hands over her soft, small feet, and then began firmly massaging the bottom of her right foot with my thumb, moving it in a circular motion. I must have hit a nerve, because Sofia exhaled and then released a deep moan that spoke to my soul.

"Oh, that feels so good."

That was all the encouragement I needed to continue and give the left foot equal attention.

"When I was young, I used to do this for my mother. She worked in a hospital for over twenty years. She would come home exhausted from working a double. I always managed to stay awake until she arrived. My father worked a lot. When he did come home, he just ate and slept. He was a brick mason. He helped build a lot of bridges and buildings throughout New York. My two older brothers and sister were into their own thing, but I always worried about my mother. I was her baby.

"I would wait for her to get good and settled on the couch or in bed, and then massage her feet. At first, she guided me through it so I'd perform to her liking, but after awhile, she didn't have to say a word. Within minutes, she'd be sound asleep."

I then looked over at Sofia. Her eyes were closed and head tilted to the side. As I stared, I imagined wedding bells and us moving out of New York and into a house in New Jersey where we could raise our children.

My mother always asked when I'd settle down, get married, and raise a family. My oldest brother said I'd never find a good woman in New York. I needed to come south and find someone with good southern values like his wife. My father said at thirty-three, I should grow up and be a man, stop dreaming so much, become more responsible. My other brother could care less; he had his own problems to worry about. But my sister would always stick up for me and tell them I needed time. Maybe now I could finally make my family proud by introducing them to Sofia.

My thoughts were interrupted when we hit a bump that

caused Sofia to jump up out of her sleep. We were in the Bronx. She sat up straight, put on her sandals, and gave the cabdriver some final instructions. I hated that the cab ride was coming to an end.

We turned down her block and pulled up in front of the building where Sofia lived. It was shortly after midnight and she was still looking like a princess, even in her intoxicated state. This definitely wasn't a Cinderella fairytale.

"Pues, mi amor, buenas noches. Hasta mañana." *(Well, my love, good night. See you tomorrow).* It was a line I'd been practicing for days. "Thanks for inviting me out. I—"

"Don't be silly, silly," Sofia said, cutting me off. "You came this far; you might as well come in."

It was a generous invitation that only a fool would've turned down. Because I was feeling so lucky, I damn near gave the cabdriver double the fare. The smile on his face showed his appreciation.

As we stepped out, my natural instincts kicked in and told me to scan the area for any unfriendly faces. I was a long way from Bedstuy, and even though Sofia had previously informed me

The

 ECollection 159

that Angel lived in Queens, I still had to take precautions. Some men's egos never allow them to let go or get over a woman.

To my surprise, there weren't many people out on this side of the block, just a few spectators hanging out of their windows and in front of their building.

Nothing out of the ordinary, I thought.

We took the elevator to the fourth floor. Once inside the apartment, Sofia wasted no time taking off her sandals and cutting on the air conditioners in the living room and bedroom. The living room was connected to the kitchen. Although it was a small one-bedroom, it was well furnished, with many pictures posted on the walls. To my surprise, I didn't notice any pictures of Angel.

Maybe their breakup is final, I thought.

She told me to make myself at home, and I planned to do just that. When she came back into the living room, she asked, "Can I get you anything?"

"I'm good."

"Do you mind if I take a quick shower. I hate feeling sweaty."

"Not at all."

"Okay, I'll be just a few minutes. Help yourself to anything in the fridge." Then she disappeared into the bathroom.

I browsed around, carefully observing everything in sight. I then heard the shower come on and couldn't help to imagine how Sofia looked naked. I walked over and took a look inside the fully stocked fridge. However, I wasn't looking for anything to eat or drink; my appetite was for Sofia.

As I walked back into the living room, I looked at my watch, not for anything in particular, just as a gesture to prepare myself for what I was thinking. I wanted to know if Sofia was as good in bed as she was on the dance floor, and there was only one way to find out. It was either now or never, and I couldn't count on her to make the first move.

I entered the candle-lit bathroom, closed the door behind me, and inhaled the sweet fragrance of Bath & Body Works. Marc Anthony's soothing voice was coming through the speakers of a small CD/radio player sitting on a shelf. I could see Sofia in silhouette through the sliding glass door. She must've felt my presence because she stopped what she was doing and faced me.

I walked over and slid open the glass door. The expression on Sofia's face indicated that she was surprised to see me standing there completely nude, but she didn't give me the impression that she wanted me to leave. In fact, she stepped to the side, as if to let me in.

Once inside, she handed me a bottle of milk and honey shower gel. I poured some onto my hand as well as her back and chest, handed it back, and then began rubbing it all over her upper body. She laughed, then poured some in her hand and a little on *my* back and chest before placing the gel on the shower rack. She then rubbed it on my upper body, as well. We then did the same for the lower parts of our body.

We massaged each other thoroughly with the liquid soap: neck, shoulders, arms, chest, breasts, stomach, back, legs, ass, feet, shaved crotch, and the shaft of my hard on. We then rubbed our slippery bodies together, heightening our sensual mood. The warm water showered down on us, washing away the soapy suds.

Sofia looked up at me with soft, sleepy eyes, and her mouth met mine. As we kissed, I placed my dick between her thighs, stimulating her clit. I cupped her right breast and sucked on her nipple, letting the water overflow my mouth. I then turned

her around and slid the length of my bat between her mittens,

while gently pulling her wet hair, causing her head to fall back,

fully exposing her neck. I attacked the side of her neck with my

tongue, pressed it deep into her flesh, and worked my way down

to her shoulders.

She reached behind and stroked my manhood as it rested

between her soft cheeks. The sensation caused me to throw *my*

head back, letting the water splash down on my face. It was

definitely time to take our intimate rain dance on dry land, the

bedroom.

We stepped out of the shower, and Sofia quickly reached

for a towel, but I took her by the hand, pulled her close to me,

and began sucking the water off every inch of her body. I started

at her neck then worked my way down.

By the time I reached her thighs, Sofia pulled away and

said in a weak voice, "Wait, Papi, let's go in my room."

I smiled and complied with her request. After drying our

bodies, Sofia turned off the CD, blew out the candle, and led me

into her bedroom.

The room was cool due to the air conditioner, but I was definitely about to warm things up a bit. She turned on the TV to provide some light, but muted the sound. Latin music could be heard from an apartment nearby. I wanted to learn everything that pleased Sofia, and at one in the morning, I was sure to be her late night chocolate fix.

We climbed on the bed and began kissing. Her fair skin against my dark complexion was like night and day. She was my sun and I was her moon and stars. We were no longer in the Bronx, but alone in San Juan, lying on white sand under a palm tree. The clear blue water came ashore, dampening our feet.

I sucked on her bottom lip, and then worked my way down to her erect nipples, which were the size of jelly beans. I had to explore the rest of her body, and began to lick, suck, and kiss my way down to her pink polished pedicure. Sofia's mouth fell open and released a deep sigh as I sucked on her right big toe and slid my tongue between the others.

I wanted to turn her over and lick her back and behind her legs, but decided against it. I wanted to leave some parts of her body untouched for later. Instead, I moved up to between her thighs, and then licked my lips as if I was about to indulge in a tasty meal, a butter-pecan-Rican treat. As I pressed my tongue against the folds of Sofia's flesh, she arched her back and grabbed hold of her sheets, as to brace herself for what was about to transpire. I took her into my mouth, wrapped my lips around her clitoris, and sucked on it as if it was a nipple.

"Aye, Papi, it feels so good."

She had me at, "Aye, Papi." I didn't need any over-the-counter prescriptions or false hope remedies to help keep me going. Hearing her say those two words, "Aye, Papi," was my Spanish Fly.

Her sweet juices flowed down the back of my throat, and each time I swallowed, it caused me to pull on her even tighter. She threw her hips up at me and grabbed the back of my head, pulling me deeper into her. I used my tongue to massage her, as my bottom lip slid in and out of her wet pussy.

I held her legs up, and then slid my tongue just below her wet opening. I threw her legs up even higher so I could go where I was sure no man had gone before. I nearly suffocated myself as I buried my face between her soft cheeks. She became possessed by a foreign spirit and spoke in her native tongue.

"Aye, Papi, pon tu grande pinga negro dentro de mi."

Sofia's body became tense, and then she released a flood of emotions all over my face. I came up for air and rubbed her fluids into my skin like lotion. She lay there trying to regain control of her body.

"Damn, baby, I…I don't wanna move."

"Just lay there, Mami. Let me do all the work."

I then climbed up on Sofia and rubbed the head of my dick on her sensitive clit. Her body squirmed. Her sweet moans and groans were like music to my ears, and I was definitely moving to the beat as I pumped faster and harder.

"Put it in, baby," she begged nearly out of breath, and I did as I was told.

I held myself in a pushup position, lifted my left leg a few inches off the bed, and started moving my body into hers like a snake, going deeper until I traveled eight inches deep into her exotic garden. We got so caught up in the heat of passion that neither one of us bothered to ask for a condom. I wasn't planning on using one anyway. I told myself that if I ever got this opportunity, I would make it a lifetime experience, and getting Sofia pregnant would confirm that.

I threw her legs up over my shoulders, rested on my knees, scooped her ass up like ice cream, and went to work. I reached the point of no return and couldn't hold back any longer. Sofia and I came at the same time. We released a soulful Latin melody not even Carlos Santana's guitar could fuck with. My body collapsed on hers, and then I rolled over onto my back. Chests heaving, bodies warm and sweaty, we nearly exhausted ourselves.

Calmness came over me and my eyelids became heavy. My mind was thinking of round two, but my body had other plans. Just as I was about to fall into a deep sleep, I heard pounding at Sofia's front door and my eyelids flew open. My entire body came alive, and before I could turn to Sofia, she had already jumped out of bed.

"Who the fuck is that?" I asked, but knew the answer.

Sofia didn't respond. Instead, she put on some shorts and a t-shirt, and left me in bed. I walked out into the living room where my clothes were and put them back on. The person wouldn't let up as he tried to break down the door.

"Sofia, open this fuckin' door! I know you got somebody in there!"

How the fuck did he know that? I thought. *Damn nosey ass neighbors.*

It was Angel. It was obvious that Sofia had some unfinished business to deal with. She turned to me with fear in her eyes. She then looked at the window that led to the fire escape, and I looked at her as if she had lost her damn mind. I'm no Muhammad Ali, but I have a serious knuckle game. I can handle my own. *Bedstuy* do or die. I didn't expect it to happen this way, but figured this night would be as good as any to prove my love. I planned to leave the same way I came, through the front door.

To Be Continued…

Cake

I figured the best way to stop thinking about my ex-girlfriend was to hang out with my road dawgs, two cool brothers who worked at the WJDM radio station in Elizabeth, New Jersey: Bobby Butler, a professional DJ, and his intern, Chad Moss, a Kean University student. It was the summer of 2007, and we were out celebrating Chad's birthday.

"I thought about asking you to hang out with us," DJ Bobby Butler said as I sat in the front of his Suburban. "I just didn't know how your fiancée felt about letting you out of her sight."

Right then and there, I had the opportunity to set the record straight, but I didn't. I could have told my friend that I was having second thoughts about getting married because I couldn't get over Kay Parker, even though I had given an engagement ring to Sara Best, the fine sister who was supposed to make me forget about Kay, my ex. Instead, I played Macho Man, that brother who had his life all together.

"Sara is a beautiful woman," Chad said from the backseat, telling me something that everybody knew.

"Thank you, my man," I replied, acknowledging the compliment like I really had something to do with Sara's natural beauty.

"Fine-looking sista," Bobby agreed. "Still, we got to throw you a bachelor party."

I laughed. "You think I need a bachelor party?"

"All dawgs that walk down that path need a bachelor party," Bobby told me. "Just to let them know they won't be getting any more new pussy."

"New pussy?" Chad spoke up. "I ain't even getting any old pussy. I ain't getting jack."

"Come on, Chad," Bobby said. "Good looking, slim brother like you, you should be throwing it down each and every night, twice on Sundays."

"Not in my world, Bobby."

"Sad," Bobby moaned. "Oh, so sad. Isn't it sad, Tommy?"

"He got time," I said, serving up a weak defense for the

college boy. "Chad is a young stud."

"That's even more reason for him to not waste time," Bobby came back. "I would introduce Chad to some sistas I know, but all the chicks I know are scandalous. What Chad needs is a nice college girl."

"What's wrong with scandalous?" Chad seriously wanted to know, like he thought getting pussy was just getting pussy.

Bobby laughed. "Chad, you don't take scandalous home to mother."

"Right now, I could use scandalous," Chad told us. "Guys, I could really use scandalous. Mother doesn't have to know jack."

Bobby and I had to laugh at that because Chad sounded so hopeless, so out to sea.

"Well, I guess we have to go with scandalous, being it's your birthday and all." Bobby replied, and then punched in some numbers on his car phone.

"Hello." A soft female voice filled the air. Bobby had her on speakerphone so Chad and I could hear everything.

"It's the Big Man."

"I heard you on the radio this morning."

"I didn't think you got up that early, Miss Lady."

"I was still in bed, but I was listening. I love the sound of your voice, Big Man. It's like you're whispering in my ear."

"You don't sound too bad yourself."

"What you want, baby?"

"Why you think I want something?"

"You only call this early when you want something. I know you, Bobby."

"I'm calling for a friend."

"A friend in need?"

"You down for it?"

"It depends on what you have in mind, baby. I worked a double last night. My feet were burning up. You know how energetic my show is."

"You got to come down off those high stiletto heels."

"I would, but you men like them too much."

"You know I like bare feet."

"Yeah, you do. I really enjoyed that pedicure you gave me the last time you were here. You made my feet feel good. As a matter of fact, you made me feel good all over."

"Real horny?"

"That, too. It was nice. A lot of men don't know how to take their time with a lady."

"It's real easy with a hot lady like you."

"Flattery will get you everything. But seriously, what's up?"

"You mean besides my dick?"

"You get turned on that easy with me just talking to you?"

"You got that smooth, sexy voice, Miss Lady. You should be on the radio, 'round midnight, but you'd probably be too hot for the FCC."

"You're funny."

"You got any plans for this afternoon?"

"I'm home until I have to work tonight. You want to come over? Spend some time?"

"Only if you let me freak you."

"You freak me; I freak you. What's the difference?"

"I'm traveling with my dawgs this afternoon."

"I thought you wanted to freak, baby?"

"I do."

"You have the wrong lady here; I don't do threesomes. One-on-one is my thing."

"I got Tommy Gunn with me."

"You on speakerphone, Bobby?"

"Yeah?"

"Hey, Tommy. I want you to come see me. I've wanted you to check out my crib for the longest. You know I'm a lady with class."

"And a big round ass!"

"Bobby, you need to stop. I don't want Tommy to think I'm some nasty nympho."

"Tommy likes nasty nymphos."

"Well, I'd rather hear Tommy speak for himself. I mean, there's a time to be nasty and time to be nice."

"You nice and nasty today?"

"It depends on who I'm with. Y'all coming over? I want y'all to come over."

"I got a birthday boy with me."

"It's Tommy's birthday?"

"Not Tommy's. It's Chad's birthday."

"Do I know Chad?"

"Not yet. He's the new intern at the radio station, a college boy."

"Maybe he can teach me something."

"I'm thinking you could teach him something about anatomy and physiology."

"I do know a little something about the human body."

"I was hoping you'd say that."

"Where are you at now, Bobby?"

"In your neighborhood."

"Okay, let me go so I can put some clothes on."

"Don't put on too many now."

"I'm feeling you, baby."

After hanging up, Bobby glanced over his shoulder and told Chad, "That was Cake, dawg."

I was always amused when Bobby Butler used Hip Hop slang like "dawg". Bobby never broadcasted his age, but with all his experience in radio, his three ex-wives, and five children, I knew he had to be in his late thirties or early forties, a lot older than myself at twenty-five and the other guys we hung out with.

But the man was down to earth, and I never passed up a chance to hang out with him.

We met at a strip club in Newark, New Jersey, where he introduced me to Cake.

"You know why they call her 'Cake'?" Bobby Butler asked me that night while we were both hanging out at the V.I.P. Lounge.

I shook my head, mesmerized by the moves of that sexy dancer. All she wore were a pair of baby blue thongs. I sat in a black leather chair, like the one Bobby Butler sat in across from me. He had taken a liking to me and paid for the lap dances we enjoyed at the club.

We couldn't touch the dancers per club policy, but she could rub her long, brown body all over us. I didn't like the super confident attitude of the dancer, but I had to admit that she knew how to do her thing, work her show. She was eye candy and had my dick as hard as Chinese mathematics. Then Bobby asked me why I thought they called her Cake.

"Show my new friend why they call you 'Cake'," Bobby instructed the dancer, who seemed to enjoy shaking her round ass in my face. To make it real nasty, the private dancer pulled on her thong and made the material go even deeper into the deep crack of her bouncing bottom, leaving almost nothing to the imagination. "Touch her ass," he whispered to me.

"No, man," I said, although I couldn't keep my eyes off that wiggling, dark brown, perfectly round ass. "You know the rules. I don't want to get kicked out of here."

"Touch it. Go 'head. She won't say anything."

I was still reluctant, but encouraged because the lap dancer looked over her shoulder and winked at me. I reached out and touched that ass. It was soft, smooth, and warm. She moved it up and down on the palms of my hands. I felt like she was pouring her Jell-O like ass into the bowl that was my hands.

"Soft as cake," Bobby whispered, and I had to agree.

There were other nights I hung out with Bobby, and most of those nights we spent at strip clubs. If there was a new strip club in the area, Bobby knew about it.

That wasn't the only time I saw Cake. I even had a few conversations with her, always at a club, but she always had some kind of attitude, like she was too much of a diva to speak to me, like I was some strip club trick. Even with all that, Bobby was convinced the dancer had a "thing" for me.

I couldn't believe that, because Cake called me a "pretty boy," like I was some soft, sorry sucker. In return, I called her a "nasty nympho," because she acted like she was on a mission to seduce every man she encountered.

Cake prided herself on giving the best lap dances in the business.

"I know how to do my thing," Cake once told me.

On that night, I was sitting in the backseat of Bobby's sleek ride; Cake was riding in the front and had to turn in her seat to talk to me. It was late, after all the clubs had closed. She had talked Bobby into dropping her off at her home. I wanted to go to sleep. I didn't want any drama, and all Cake was about 24/7 was the drama. As I slumped down in the backseat, I really didn't want to hear her yapping.

"Shake it real good, baby," Cake boasted. "Make a stud bust a nut in his pants." Then she smiled like that was some big accomplishment.

I promised myself right then and there that it wouldn't

happen to me. I would never allow myself to get so worked up behind her booty-clapping ass that I lose control, soiling myself with my own semen. Because Cake loved a challenge, I was determined to resist her. And if we ever did get together, which I seriously doubted at that time, I knew I had to be the one calling the shots. Call me a "control freak" or whatever. I just knew that letting a female like Cake get the upper hand would be a move I would forever regret.

That afternoon, Cake greeted us at the door of her apartment in a leopard print jumpsuit. It was obvious even to the casual admirer that she had nothing on beneath it, but perfumed body lotion. Her back was bare down to the crack of her ass, and her cleavage in the front was also on display. She had brushed her long hair back and pulled it into a long ponytail.

I thought Cake looked more elegant than she had any right to be. I also had to admit that I was player hating, trying hard to bring her down to the gutter where I thought all "nasty nymphos" deserved to be. However, after stepping into her apartment, I had to acknowledge her taste and class.

I had to give Cake her props; her crib was laid. In the

living room were Crate & Barrel sofas and end tables, a stone fireplace, thick carpeting, smoked glass tables, and large floor-to-ceiling windows. Although the cream-colored furniture was sparse, the furnishing was just right in her immaculate space. It was like stepping into a place called Tranquility. It was top shelf from the furnishings to the elaborate sound system that spit out smooth jazz throughout the room.

As for the hostess, Chad's expression said it all. His jaw dropped down to his socks when he saw Cake. Her body was outstanding, clothed or naked.

Once, on the car speakerphone with Bobby, and me right there in the front seat, she told him, "My grandma is responsible for this body. She fed me cheese grits and eggs, sausage, and country bacon. That's how I start my day now, no matter what time I get up. And I can really throw down on some fried chicken and potato salad. Got to get dem homemade biscuits, too."

But that was only part of her story.

"I was on the basketball team," Cake went on. "I was a cheerleader, and I always loved dancing."

From her spacious living room, I could peek into the

kitchen. The sparkling kitchen equipment impressed me with its Viking stove and Sub Zero brand refrigerator. The dining area was a round glass table with tall black and cream-colored chairs. Taking it all in for the first time, I had to shake my head, amazed. I didn't realize that dirty dancers had it like that.

"Who is this handsome young man?" Cake wanted to know, smiling at Chad as we moved into her place. She was all in the college boy's face, but Chad was too taken with her to step back. From where he stood frozen like that, I knew he could smell her fresh breath.

"This is Chad," Bobby told her as he took off his jacket. I didn't take off anything because I didn't want to get too comfortable in this hoe's house. I told myself I was only there because I was curious about how she lived away from the strip clubs that were her second homes in New Jersey and New York.

Cake closed the door behind us, and then said, "Hello, Chad. I'm glad you could come see me."

Chad was awestruck, like he had never seen a pretty woman before. He couldn't seem to find his voice as he looked from me to Bobby. "You're beautiful," he finally blurted out.

He made me feel embarrassment for him, like he was playing the fool for Cake. Bobby Butler didn't help matters by laughing out loud at Chad's predicament.

I sat on the couch and looked down at Cake's feet. The pedicure was impeccable, the nails painted a bright red to match her lipstick. Her feet sank into the thick cream-colored carpet, and I had to resist the urge to take off my Timbs. I didn't want to be the one responsible for dirtying up Cake's place. It was obvious that she took pride in her surroundings, and for some strange reason, that made me hate her more.

"I'm so glad you think I'm beautiful, Chad. You see Bobby and Tommy take me for granted. They've seen me on my job. They want to believe that's all there is to me."

"You got to be a dancer," Chad said with adoring eyes.

"Do you have a problem with that?"

"No...no...not really," Chad stuttered, then blushed.

Cake ran a finger up and down the valley of her cleavage. "That's good, Chad. Because I don't make any excuses for what I do. I'm an entertainer, and I'm good at what I do."

That was when Cake reached out and touched Chad's

smooth, clean-shaven face. Suddenly, I realized Chad Moss was nothing but a kid. A college student, but still a kid. He had no win when it came to a worldly woman like Cake. He was totally smitten, trapped like a fly caught in a spider's web.

"Your face is as smooth as a baby's butt," Cake told Chad. "You brought me a baby, Bobby. How old is this boy? How old are you, baby?"

"Nineteen," Chad replied, with as much pride as he could muster.

"I bet you can't even get into a strip club."

Chad blushed. "I'd try to get in one to see you."

Cake continued to stroke his face. "I wouldn't want you to come, Chad. Too many bad men in there like Bobby and Tommy. They don't have any respect for women like me."

"We don't have much time," Bobby told her.

Cake nodded like she understood what he meant, but to me, it was like they were speaking in code. She turned and walked out of the room. I couldn't help but notice the roundness of her leopard-print covered ass.

Bobby followed behind her, and they disappeared

somewhere deep into the apartment.

Chad sat down on the couch beside me. "Man, Cake is too much."

I didn't know what to say to that. All I knew was that I was irritated he was so impressed with her.

It wasn't long before Bobby came back into the living room. He had a big smile on his face. In his hand, he held a CD. I knew what CD it was because I once had a copy myself. It was Mack Man's debut CD, *The Return of The Mack*.

"A little music," Bobby said as he held up the CD. On the cover was the rapper Mack Man, flanked by Goldie and Pretty Toni, his female dancers. The CD was released when Mack Man was twenty-three years old. At that time, they called him the "West Coast rapper with East Coast appeal."

Bobby handed the CD cover to me before he went to Cake's sound system. On the cover was Mack Man with his natural, shoulder-length black hair, thick mustache, slim, muscular body, bare chest with suspenders, and black leather pants. Goldie and Pretty Toni wore red leather halter-tops, red leather shorts, and red leather thigh-high boots. The first sound out of the speakers was the hardcore version of "Hands Down".

Chad smiled broadly, jumping up and down on the couch like a kid at the circus. He smiled at me, then Bobby. But his biggest smile was for Cake when she came back into the room.

Cake wore a bodysuit that was nothing but a strip of electric chiffon material. It had a halter neck, but left the sides of her torso and all of her back bare. Around her slim hips was a pair of low-riding hot pants. On her feet were blue leather shoes. She came back into the room dancing, if you could call it that. It was more like frantic undulation. Everything on Cake shook.

Through the sheer chiffon, I could see her breasts and the dark circles of her aroused nipples. She had on green eye makeup and green lipstick. Her eyes were outlined in dark mascara. She moved toward Chad like he was the only man in the room. She brought to my mind a shark going after innocent prey.

Without a word, Cake danced over to the college intern and pulled him up to his feet. She used her long body like a paintbrush, painting a masterpiece on the canvas of Chad's fully clothed body. But, of course, Cake couldn't leave it at that. She unbuttoned his shirt down to the last button. Then, she opened his shirt and ran her hands up and down his bare chest.

Chad moaned as Cake teased his nipples with her fingertips. Then, she moved her hands down to his pants and unbuckled his belt. With the boldness of a veteran lap dancer, she ran her hands up and down Chad's covered crotch and thighs. She didn't stop until she made his dick hard, then she turned and rubbed her ass against his crotch. He held her around the waist, his hands together on her flat belly as she rubbed all up against him.

I had to adjust myself in my pants because Cake was putting on a hot show.

Cake made her ass cheeks clap, as she looked over her shoulder to see how Chad was reacting. It was obvious she had his full attention. That was when she unbuttoned her pants and pushed them ever so slowly down her hips. In the back, her bodysuit was nothing but a thin strip of material that almost disappeared into the deep crack of her round, brown ass. Before we could get too happy with the view, Cake pulled her short pants up. She then turned to us, but left the pants unbuttoned.

With her hands, she pulled the straps of her bodysuit

together until the material was just a strip between her bare breasts. Then, she shook her big, well-shaped, natural breasts at us. Suddenly, she covered herself and came toward Chad.

Cake grabbed Chad's hand and sucked on one of his fingers. Not satisfied with that, she took three of his fingers into her mouth. She sucked those fingers and hummed around them. I couldn't help but think what her mouth would feel like on my hard-on. And I hated myself for that, because I felt I was being manipulated by the exotic dancer, like I had no control.

Still, I couldn't take my eyes off her and what she was doing to Chad. She took him by the hand and led him to a comfortable cream-colored armchair. She arranged him with his legs spread wide and his hands behind his head. The young intern may never have gone to a strip club, but Cake gave him an education that he couldn't have gotten anywhere else. She smiled at Bobby and me as she backed that ass up against Chad. She didn't stop until she made him cum in his pants.

By that time, I had about all that I could take. There was no way I was coming in my pants. There was no way I'd let Cake humiliate me like that.

I jumped up and said, "We got to get out of here."

Chad sat in the chair, devastated. "Oh, no. Oh, no," he moaned, looking down at his wet lap.

Cake looked over at me with a smirk on her face. "Bobby, take Chad to the bathroom so he can clean himself up."

A smiling Bobby Butler led an embarrassed Chad Moss out of the room.

"You fuckin' satisfied?" I asked Cake after the bathroom door slam shut.

"No," Cake told me, that smirk still on her face.

"What do you fuckin' want, you nasty nympho?"

"I want your fuckin' dick in me," Cake replied, while pushing a hand into the front of her pants.

"Fuck you," I said, letting her know there was no way I was going to be a sucker for her. I tried to turn away from her, but Cake was really working her hand inside the front of her pants. I stood there and refused to turn away because it was like a game then, a test of wills. When she finally took her hand out of her pants, she waved it beneath my nose.

I slapped her hand away from my face.

Cake laughed.

But I did smell it, her hot, ripe pussy.

When Bobby and Chad came back into the living room, I was the first one out of the front door.

After we dropped Chad off at his parents' house, I turned toward Bobby Butler with mad attitude. "Man, what was that shit about at that hoe's house?" I snapped.

Bobby smiled at me like I was one of his children, and then pulled out into city traffic. "Dawg, Chad had the time of his life. This is a birthday he will never forget."

"You embarrassed him, Bobby! He soiled his pants!"

"Like I said, a good time was had by all, except maybe you."

"I'm supposed to applaud what went down at Cake's crib?"

"I wanted to cheer Chad up. I do believe he's cheered up. But I don't think what's irritating you has anything to do with Chad or me."

"What do you think is irritating me?"

"I can see it all over your face, Tommy. It's too bad that

you can't. Not now anyway."

"You my head doctor now?"

"I'm nobody's psychiatrist, but I know a lot about denial. I've been there, big time, dawg."

"What am I in denial about?"

"The way you really feel about Kay Parker. Kay has got you; she's got you good. I'm just real sorry you convinced Sara that you were ready for marriage. You may be ready for marriage, but not with Sara Best."

"You're saying that I should go back to Kay?"

"Tommy, I'm saying you never left. Kay's got your nose so wide open you could drive a Mack truck through it."

I didn't say anything because I knew I was guilty as charged. I let Kay effect me like no other woman; I had let Kay touch my heart and I hadn't been the same since.

"I have to admit Kay is hot," Bobby continued, like we were just having a general conversation. But we both knew everything he said about my ex-girlfriend was like a bullet in my heart.

"Man, you don't have to tell me that."

"Kay's got a nice ass, too."

I tried to laugh at that last remark, because it was so off the wall. I just knew that Bobby couldn't be serious. Or could he? His eyes were tight on me, and he wasn't smiling.

"A real nice ass. And she don't mind showing it."

"What the fuck are you talking about?" I had to know, and I, too, was not smiling. As a matter of fact, I was ready to kick his ass, friend or no friend. I really didn't like him coming out of his face like that, talking about my ex-girl's ass.

"Last night, Tommy. At The New Club House. There was a Best Butt Contest. Kay dropped her panties and won it."

The anger came up hot and fast in me. "You're joking, right?"

"No joke, dawg. I'm telling you because it sounds a whole lot better coming from a friend. I know she's no longer your girl, but there might be some residual feeling there. As a matter of fact, we both know there is. I'm telling you like this because I know you. Somebody might mention this to you in general conversation, and, knowing your temper, you would take it as an insult, like you still have some say over what that girl does with her body."

I shook my head, not believing that Kay would show
her ass in public. I looked hard into my friend's face and saw no
deception there. I worked my bottom lip, trying hard to hold
onto my rage, but I really wanted to shout at someone, call
someone a liar. I was frustrated because I knew that someone
wouldn't be Bobby Butler.

"Don't take it so hard, dawg," Bobby advised me. "It was
all in fun."

"You know nothing like that would've gone down if I had
been there."

"I know that, but you weren't there. You've moved on.
You're about to be married. Let her move on. Let it go."

I knew he was right, but I couldn't let it go. "Who was
Kay with?" I had to know.

Bobby looked at me with much compassion. "No dude,
dawg. She seemed to be on a ladies' night out. She shared a booth
with three fly looking sistas. One of them had green eyes. She was
also in the Best Butt Contest, the only real competition your girl
had."

I really wanted to punch something, kick something, to unleash the dragon, but somehow I managed to keep my cool. Kay showing her ass in public? What kind of shit was that?

I tried to tell myself that it was none of my business, but the thought just wouldn't take root. All I could think about was Kay Parker showing the world something only I was supposed to see. I'll never forget that time in her crib when she told me that she was mine, forever.

Now Bobby Butler, my best friend, the radioman, was telling me that I wasn't the only man to see that entire bootilicious splendor. But I was cool. Or at least I tried to be on the outside. Inside, my blood boiled and I wanted to break out of my skin.

How could you do that, Kay? I needed to ask her. *Share what was mine with the entire world? What were you drinking? Were you doing drugs? Were you trying to attract a new lover?* I had too many questions, and the only one that could answer them was Kay Parker.

"You have to calm down, dawg," Bobby told me, and I knew he was right. "Move on beyond this."

I didn't say anything else to Bobby as we drove back to the radio station, where I left my ride. We got out of his car, facing the back of the WJDM building. I said goodbye, and then watched him walk into the building.

I climbed into my Navigator. Because I only used my cell phone for emergencies, and because emergencies were so few and far in between, I always had to search through my vehicle when I needed to make a call. When I finally found my little phone, which was pressed in between some car registration paperwork, I punched in the number.

When she answered, she sounded sad and distant. "Hello."

I came out salty. "What is this shit about you showing your ass in public?"

Kay came back with a stinger. "That's my business."

"Is it true?"

"Forget you!"

"Tell me, Kay! Is it true?"

"I said forget you, Tommy!"

"Have you lost your damn mind?"

"Don't you curse at me! Don't you dare curse at me! You don't run me, Tommy Gunn. Try that possessive shit with your fiancée."

"Now who's cursing?"

"I'm not cursing! I don't consider 'shit' a curse!"

"What is it then?"

"It's some strong language I'm directing at your sorry ass!"

"I'm sorry now?"

"Yeah, you're sorry! I don't hear anything from you for two months, and then you call me about some silly shit!"

"Why, Kay? Why did you do that, enter that contest at the club?"

"Tommy, it is really none of your business! What gossipy, nosey ass told you?"

"Don't worry about that!"

"I'm not worried about anything when it comes to you! I think the whole thing is really silly! You going on and on about something that has nothing to do with you. I am a single, black woman who doesn't have to answer to anyone!"

"You pulled your panties down and showed your bare

ass!"

"Yes, I did!"

"To win some silly Best Butt Contest!"

"Yes, I did!"

"What in the hell did you think you were proving?"

"Who has the best booty."

"Besides that?"

"Nothing besides that, Tommy. This is really not deep at all. You're making a big deal out of it by going on and on about it. I won some money; it's over. End of story."

"I guess now you're getting ready for the Best Butt Finals?"

"You're trying to be funny, but I'm really not amused. Forget you, Tommy. You asked me a question, and I answered your question. End of conversation."

"You hanging up on me now?"

"Tommy, what else is there to say?"

"I don't know."

"That's what I figured you'd say. Leave me alone, Tommy. We had some good times. Now leave it at that."

"I miss you, Kay."

"Don't go there, Tommy. Not as long as you have a fiancée. She would really be hurt if she knew you were talking to me. I have no desire to hurt that girl. She never did anything to me."

"So you're the bigger person now?"

"You're the one that hurt me. You're the one that hurt me so bad because of your cheating ass."

"I'm sorry, Kay."

"I'm sorry, too. But nothing you can say or do will make me forget that hurt, Tommy."

"I never wanted to hurt you."

"But you did. I'll get over it, Tommy. I have no choice. You took that out of my hands by judging me as some kind of freak that you couldn't take seriously. I may be a little freaky in the bedroom, but I never cheated on you and I did love you. I loved you as hard as I could. I'm just sorry it wasn't enough for you to take me seriously."

"Let's get together. Let's talk."

"That's not a good idea, Tommy."

"Why not?"

"If we got together, we'd talk for a little while."

"That's all I want."

"But it wouldn't end there, Tommy. I'd want to feel you inside me. You know that wouldn't be right. I refuse to play myself like that by starting something I know I can't finish. And I refuse to hurt that girl just for a quick fuck."

"It's always been more than that between us."

"You're talking about the past, Tommy. Who knows what would happen now?"

"And, of course, you don't want to take that chance."

"Not with your new girl in the picture."

"What if I break off the engagement?"

"If you do, when you do that, maybe we'll have something to talk about."

I knew there was nothing more to say, but I just didn't want to hang up. It took Kay to break the connection. As I sat there in my ride, no one had to tell me that I had done the wrong thing. Reaching out to Kay solved nothing. All it really did was increase the pressure in me to the point where I felt like I was about to explode for real. I didn't need to talk to Kay; I needed to make love to her.

What that would solve, I didn't know, but my hunger for her was so intense that it actually caused me some physical discomfort. My heart ached, my head ached, and there was heaviness in my groin that caused me all kinds of irritation. I felt I had no real life unless I could build a bridge back to Kay. *I have to do something,* I thought as I sat in my Lincoln Navigator.

Soon, I was on the road.

I knocked on the door and it opened.

Cake looked me up and down. "I knew you'd be back." She stood in a formfitting, gold t-shirt with a picture of Bob Marley in red on the front of it. Covering her hips was low hanging bottoms. Her pretty feet were bare.

"You gonna let me in?" I asked.

Saying nothing, Cake opened the door wider. I walked pass her, brushing against her breasts as I went into the living room. My brief, accidental contact with her let me know she wore no bra beneath her t-shirt. She closed the door behind me, and then stretched like she had just awakened from a nap.

"Were you sleeping?" I asked.

"A little nap," she admitted. "Things got a little boring after you guys left. How's Chad?"

I became indignant, feeling that she was making fun of Chad. "You know what you did to him."

"I made him happy, made this birthday one to remember. I really had to search to find that particular CD; I was never really into Mack Man. C.J. Smooth is the rapper that I really like."

"I'm a big C. J. Smooth fan, too. I like to call him 'The Smooth One'."

"You wanna hear some Smooth?"

"You gonna have to search for him?"

"Not for Smooth. Although he hasn't recorded anything new, I still play his old stuff. Sit. Make yourself at home."

"I can't stay long."

"You brothers never do."

I watched her ass in the denim bikini bottom as she moved around the room. She went to the entertainment center to put on C.J. Smooth's debut CD.

Cake looked over her shoulder. "You brothers just like to

come up here to do your business, then split. I'm cool with that."

"Why you let it go down like that?"

"Ain't no big thing, Tommy. I'm not looking for romance. I'm not about that. I'm too independent for that. I don't need no man to take care of me. I can take care of myself. I got money in the bank, a nice whip, a fly crib. I work hard, but when the shit gets to be too much, I go on a nice cruise."

I sat on the cream-colored couch and Cake came up behind me. She reached over the back of the couch to massage my shoulders. "I want you to enjoy yourself while you're here, Tommy. I want you to have a nice time so you'll think about coming to see me again."

I looked straight at her and let her know, "I don't pay for pussy."

Cake looked hurt. "This is not business, cutie pie," she assured me, as she pulled my jacket off my shoulders. "This is personal. Time for Cake to have some fun."

"Why me? For free?"

"You're a challenge to me, Tommy. When I was growing up in the hood, a fine brother like you wouldn't take a second look at me." In the background, C.J. Smooth's presence was made known by his rapping on one of my favorite jams, "Lesson Learned", a song you could dance to and learn from. "It's different now," she let me know. "Everything is cool now. I got you here with me now."

I had to help her pull off my t-shirt, and as I sat there with my bare chest, Cake came around the couch to stand in front of me.

"How many times a day do you change clothes?" I wanted to know, as Cake looked down at me.

"It depends on what I'm doing."

"Or who you're doing."

"Don't be mean now."

"Did Bobby pay you to dance for Chad?"

"I'm an entertainer, Tommy. Bobby only paid for a lap dance. Only as much as Chad would pay for a lap dance at the club. That has nothing to do with what we're about to do, though."

Cake was right. I should've shut my mouth, but I didn't. As Cake sank to her knees between my legs, I said, "I'm not here for a lap dance."

Cake smiled at me with a brilliance that felt like love. "I know that." She rubbed my thighs with both hands. "Haven't you ever heard of foreplay?"

I nodded, leaned back, and let Cake do her thing. She untied my Timbs and pulled them off. She massaged my feet through my socks, and then took them off. I squirmed in my seat when she rubbed my crotch, tracing the outline of my hard-on.

"What's with you and Bobby?" I wanted to know.

"B is my friend," Cake told me, as she continued to rub me through my pants.

"You fuckin' Bobby?"

That's when Cake stopped what she was doing to look me dead in my eyes. "We make love. Sometimes. When he feels up for it."

"He doesn't pay?"

"I told you, Tommy, B is my good friend. He looks out for me. He's the one who told me about the "Jersey Jazz" video shoot. I got a big part in that. It's coming out soon, and you got to check it out. It's gonna be on MTV and BET."

I became silent as Cake began to excite herself by rubbing on my hard-on. She lovingly measured the length of it with her hands. "I knew you had a big one, Tommy. I looked at those big hands and feet, and I said to myself, 'That boy is blessed.'"

I grunted a little as Cake put her hands in my pants. Her fingers felt good on my balls.

"Bobby's got a modest tool," Cake told me. "Nothing to brag about, but he knows how to work it. He gets the job done. Your tool is gonna make me moan and shout."

"I hope I don't disappoint you."

Cake smiled up at me. "You won't do that. I won't let you do that. Half the battle is getting me turned on."

"Are you turned on?"

"Big time, baby. Can't you feel my heat?"

Before I could say anything, Cake pushed my pants and briefs down. I had to lift my ass, but she did most of the work. When she saw my tool, she grabbed it with both hands.

"Oh, baby! I'm gonna have fun with this."

Cake jacked me a little, then bent her head to lick me. She teased the head, then ran her long tongue down the length

of it. Before it could get too good to me, Cake rose to her feet. "I
want you in my bed, Tommy."

I stepped out of and over my discarded briefs and pants.

The bedroom, with its big windows, was immaculate and
cream colored with highly polished dressers and bedside cabinets.
The bed was square and king sized. As I stood naked behind
Cake, she pulled the top sheet back and pushed the four pillows
onto the thick carpeting of the floor. Then, she turned toward me
and walked into my arms. I stroked her hot body and kissed her
full lips when she lifted her head to me. As I kissed her, her hands
became busy on my torso and then moved ever so gently to my
bare ass.

Cake breathed heavily as she stroked and squeezed my ass.
My hot, thick hard-on pressed into her belly. "I want it," she said,
urgently pushing into me. I could hear Smooth's "Let The Funk
Flow" playing far away in the living room. "Undress me, Tommy.
I love for a man to undress me for sex and then kiss everything he
uncovers."

I grabbed the bottom of her tee and pulled it up over her
head. She let it hit the floor as I reached for her bare breasts. They

were hot, soft, and sweet when I licked them.

Cake moaned like a woman on fire, as her breasts met my hot, wet tongue. I licked each nipple thoroughly and massaged her bare back. She emitted a deep sigh of pleasure when I pushed her onto her back and climbed up on the bed to join her. I continued to suck her nipples, while she reached out for my hard-on.

"This is what I want," Cake moaned, as she squeezed my hard-on with both her hands.

That was when I gripped her bikini bottoms and pushed them down her hot thighs. When she was totally naked, Cake pushed herself back onto the bed. Totally naked like that, she seemed totally vulnerable, as if the confident sexual entertainer had become a naked, needy Black woman. I almost felt sorry for her, like I was getting ready to take something she needed to be giving to someone else, someone who truly loved her.

We kneeled in the middle of the bed, stroking and kissing, moaning and groaning together. I rubbed her flat belly, then reached down to rub her pussy. Like many females today, Cake had shaved off all her pubic hair.

"Fuck it, baby," Cake said as I intimately fondled her, getting her juices on my fingers as I plunged my hand into her wet heat. "Fuck it now."

I looked down on her as she fell back onto the bed, her legs spread so wide that I could see her pussy and the puckered asshole beneath it. I pushed her knees back and sank between her rough thighs. The pussy was good, hot and tight, and sweet smelling as Cake threw it up at me.

With her eyes tightly shut, Cake began to talk out of her head, like she was speaking in tongues or some foreign language. I had no idea what she was saying; then again, it really didn't matter. All Cake knew was that she had me between her thighs and I was steadily banging her sugar walls.

"Let me put my legs up, Tommy! All the way up, baby! Let you get all up inside me!"

With that said, Cake threw her long dancer legs up until her bare heels were touching my shoulders. In this position, I had complete access to the pussy. I banged Cake hard and she came, hollering and screaming my name.

When it was my turn to bust a nut, Cake climbed on

top of me. She rode my hard-on, played with my nipples, and hollered like I was hurting her. She trembled and came again, but this time, I was right behind her. I busted a nut and squeezed her butter-soft ass as I tried to bury my dick into the deepest part of her warm, wet, sweet, tight pussy.

"Your dick is king," Cake said as she reluctantly got off it. With my dick semi-hard, she stroked it. "I love a big dick," she told me and, as if to show how much, she took the head into her mouth.

When Cake finally calmed down, I let her snuggle under my arm. Even then, she couldn't keep her hands still. She kept on rubbing my sweat-soaked chest. She fell asleep with her hand wrapped around my hard-on.

When I got out of bed, I pulled the sheet over her naked body. Behind me, C.J. Smooth, The Smooth One, rapped on "Nikki Love," his Hip Hop love song. I got into my clothes and got out of there.

As I sat in my ride, I thought about what had just gone down. Cake was great in the sack, but I wasn't completely satisfied. She wasn't Kay Parker, and now, more than ever, I needed Kay, the love of my life.

Thug Passion

Friday

Between suicide bombings and natural disasters, life is too short to be getting the shorter end of the deal. When I leave this world, I want to be able to say I had my share of great sex. But, lately, I've been on a serious dry spell. Well, not completely, because if you consider masturbating gratification, then I've been getting it on the regular.

My life consists of being a mother to my fifteen-year-old daughter, Raven, and work. Her father and I went our separate ways years ago. I was young and naive at the time, and he used that to his advantage. He eventually admitted that he regretted ever letting me go. Typical black male, never knowing when they have a good thing until it's gone.

I hardly get out much, but when I do, I never seem to enjoy myself. I guess the reality of turning thirty-five tomorrow is really taking its toll on my mental state. But I have everything

I ever wanted: a daughter, a career, a car, a two-level house completely furnished by IKEA and Ethan Allen, top designers' wardrobe, and two vibrators. One is a silver bullet used to stimulate my clitoris. The other is a seven-inch vibrating dildo with a tongue attached to it. This gives me double pleasure, because while the dildo is inside of me, it moves in a circular motion and the tongue massages my clit.

My girlfriend, Alexa Hunter, felt that wasn't enough. She said I needed some excitement in my life, a vacation. So, as a birthday present, she paid for the two of us to go on a ski trip for the weekend. When she first told me about it six months ago, I looked at her strangely and said, "Girl, I don't ski!" But then she gave me a detailed description of how much fun she had on the last one, which helped change my mind.

She stated that about one percent of the people who attend these weekend getaways actually ski. Everyone else shops, parties, and drinks until their hearts stop, figuratively speaking. "nHouse Entertainment be doing their thing, girl! They have people from all over on their ski trips," she said with much excitement.

So there I was, packed and ready to go. I'm glad I had a garage and didn't have to worry about leaving my X5 BMW on the street. Although I live in the suburban neighborhood of Maplewood, New Jersey, I still like to take precautions. I was also grateful that my younger sister was able to keep my daughter for the weekend. Between her husband and their two daughters, Brittany and Ashley, she has her hands full, but I'm sure she will find Raven helpful.

Looking over my "to do" list, I wanted to make sure everything was covered. I even made a note to pack my bullet vibrator with extra batteries. I hate to do things last minute, and try to be as organized as possible. That's why I purchased my snow boots and winter coat from Neiman Marcus for this trip months ago. I also made sure all my basic needs were taken care of the day before: hair done, eyebrows arched, manicure and pedicure in tact. Needless to say I looked flawless. Whenever I step out the house, I try to look my very best.

My beautician, Marty, hooked me up big time. He gave me a contemporary style that is all about being "sleek and smooth" as he put it. With a side part, Marty silkened my hair with a glossifier and used a flat iron. He gave me layers of curls so that the sides of my hair could fall freely pass my shoulders, giving my hairstyle an attitude all of its own.

After looking over my list, everything seemed to be in order. I packed all of my essentials: feminine products, disposable camera, several outfits and shoes, bathing suit, pajamas, slippers, hair and skin products. The things women have to go through to look beautiful men will never understand.

February is not only the shortest, but also one of the coldest months of the winter. There was about four inches of snow on the ground, and the temperature was ten degrees. To keep warm, I wore a cashmere turtleneck sweater tucked into a pair of denim jeans, no belt, with the bottom pants legs stuffed into my snow boats.

Noticing the time on my watch, it was twelve-thirty. The buses planned to pull out at one, so I had to put some pep in my step.

Just as that thought was crossing my mind, my cell phone went off. It was inside my pocketbook, which was on the couch in the living room. I didn't even bother looking at the caller ID because I knew it could only be one person.

"Hello," I said into the phone.

"Girl, what the hell you doing? You ain't leave yet?" Alexa asked.

My guess was right.

"I'm on my way out the door now."

"All right, well, I'm already here. Hurry your butt up."

"Okay, I'll see you in a few."

Right after hanging up with Alexa, I called a cab.

After sprinkling on some Ralph Lauren perfume, I put on some lip gloss, a pair of small diamond studded earrings, along with a white gold diamond ring on my right index finger, and then I wrapped a large wool scarf around my face. I put on my black leather three-quarter goose with matching leather insulated fitted gloves, then carefully pulled a wool hat down on my head.

I had to laugh at myself as I carried my three-piece Louis Vuitton luggage set downstairs to my cab, because I knew I would come back with more things than I initially traveled with.

After piling my luggage into the cab, I was ready to get this show on the road.

Minutes later, we pulled into a huge parking lot in Irvington Center, the location where everyone had to meet. Ten buses were lined up, waiting and ready to leave.

According to my information packet, Alexa and I were to be seated on bus two. After carefully placing my belongings in the luggage compartment beneath the bus, I boarded and immediately looked for Alexa. It wasn't hard to locate her because she was waving me down to get my attention.

According to many men, Alexa is drop-dead gorgeous, and I wouldn't disagree. She has a dark brown complexion, about a shade darker than mine, stands five-seven, and is a size eight. She was wearing blue denim jeans that hugged her hips like a lover, black leather boots with a flat heel, and a black zippered sweater with a hood. Whatever I lack in size, she made up for it, and I'm not mad at her.

I am a petite woman and proud of it. When I was coming up as a child, I was constantly picked on about my small frame, but now I'm very thankful for being a size four, sometimes a size two depending on the designer. There are so many women my age who have let their bodies go completely. The way I look at it, at five-three, my size goes well with my height.

"Girl, you was about to get left," Alexa said as she stepped out to give me the seat near the window.

"Now you know black people don't do anything on time, okay," I said in defense, while taking off my coat and scarf and placing them in the overhead compartment. I left my hat on and held onto my pocketbook.

As we were taking our seats, the bus captain began demanding our attention.

"A'ight, y'all, listen up," he spoke into the microphone. "I'ma keep this plain and simple. My name is Smooth, and I'll be your captain of this here bus. There is absolutely no smoking whatsoever on the bus or in the bathrooms or your ass will get put off. For those of you who don't know, we'll be traveling to Gettysburg, Pennsylvania, and staying at the Eisenhower Resort. This will be a three hour trip."

At least I'll be able to get a good nap in, I thought.

"If this is your first time, just so you'll know, we party as soon as the bus pulls off, and keeps it going until the end of the weekend," Smooth continued. "But most importantly, what goes on in PA…" In unison, nearly every person on the bus said, "stays in PA," and broke out in laughter.

Smooth said, "Now that's what I'm talkin' 'bout. Let's do the damn thing."

Soon after Smooth finished, Alexa whispered, "Sincere and Roc are on bus four."

Sincere is Alexa's "off again, on again" man, and Roc is someone that Alexa has been trying to get me to meet for months. She is always trying to hook me up with a guy. She's my girl and I love her dearly, but we don't have the same taste in men. She likes thugs and I prefer a gentleman. I would even date a straight up geek before thinking about dating someone who has very little respect for women or themselves.

I realized a long time ago that I didn't have to be in a relationship. There was a time when I thought I needed a man. I even told myself that by age thirty I would be married, not really caring who my husband would be, just as long as he loved me and gave me all the affection and attention I needed. But as that old cliché goes, be careful what you ask for because you just might get it. Well, I didn't get a husband, but I got one crazy ass fiancé.

To change the subject, I asked, "I thought you were going to put some weave in?"

Alexa touched her short hair and replied, "I started to, but I didn't have time. I just went and got me a doobie. It's that bad?"

"No, girl, it looks good on you."

"Thanks."

Someone yelled out Alexa's name. It was a girlfriend of hers sitting in the back of the bus. Alexa stood up and walked to the rear, leaving me alone. I couldn't help but to return my thoughts to my ex-fiancé; his name isn't important. During our relationship, he stole my happiness. He didn't love himself, and I realized back then that I didn't truly love myself either. I got tired of the mental abuse and found the strength to take my happiness back. It took me two years to get out of that relationship and another two years to get him out of my system.

I promised to never take myself or my daughter through that hardship again. I refuse to travel down the same road my mother and her mother did, staying with a man for benefits while they physically abuse your children. At least that was definitely the case with my mother. She is a woman who got lost in looking for love. We were a happy family until a man came along.

I was sheltered most of my life because my mother had two girls and didn't trust anyone. She, for the most part, was looking for someone to love, but as a teen had to play her mother's role because her father had an affair for about twenty years with other women, one of them being her mother's best friend, who ended up having two children with him. This crushed her mother's spirit, and she began drinking heavily.

My grandmother was a beautiful, caramel, small woman with long, wavy hair and a small waist that caught the eye of every man in every bar she visited, and on many occasions she faced near death experiences from hanging out in the streets.

The pressure was so heavy for my mother that she ended up dropping out of high school during her senior year so she could take care of her mother; she continued this while raising me and my sister. By this time, her mother was an alcoholic.

Growing up, I witnessed my mom fight plenty of men, whom I think were her boyfriends. I couldn't understand why her kids weren't enough to love, but she took care of us. She would play games, jump rope with us, and talk with us; it would be

so nice. Hell, sometimes kids rung our doorbell looking for my
mother to jump rope and do drills with *them*. In my eyes, we
had everything we needed, wanted, and more. My mom treated
us like precious black dolls, and made sure we were clean and
nicely dressed. We weren't abused or went hungry. We were happy
until my step-dad came into the picture. What followed was pure
neglect, along with mental and physical abuse.

My mom was a lost soul, looking for love in all the wrong
men, even my dad. But my step-dad took the cake. He was
the devil's advocate. His MO was about beating and mentally
tormenting children, especially me. Being the oldest, anything
that wasn't done fell on me.

During my teen years, I had no friends, because I had
to go straight home from school. When I didn't have school, I
wasn't allowed to go outside at all, and had to be in bed at eight
every night. I ended up spending a lot of time in front of the TV.
However, during the summers, I was fortunate enough to get a
summer job. It gave me a little freedom, but I had to save all my
money up to buy school clothes.

Because of my stepfather, I have become overprotective

of my daughter and cautious of men. I don't know much about my biological father, other than that we have similar personalities according to my mother, but I think I'm more like her. He passed away when I was young. Sometimes I wonder if my problems with men lie there.

My thoughts were interrupted by the blaring sound of Hip Hop music and loud cheers from the people on the bus. Smooth wasn't lying when he said the party starts as soon as the bus departs. People were up out of their seats, dancing in the aisle, and passing food and alcoholic beverages around. All I could do was laugh because Alexa was one of the main instigators in this party on wheels. Well, you know what they say…if you can't beat 'em, join 'em. Someone handed me a bottle of Green Apple Smirnoff Ice, and all I could do was sit back and enjoy the ride.

Three hours later, we finally arrived at our destination. Many people staggered their way off the bus because they already had too much to drink. Alexa and I got our luggage and walked into the hotel's lobby.

The Eisenhower Resort Inn is not only spacious, but immaculate and gorgeous. The staff greeted us with warm smiles, as they informed us that this is south central Pennsylvania's largest facility of its kind. The 307 beautifully appointed guestrooms offer a variety of lodging accommodations. Gettysburg is also where former President and General Dwight D. Eisenhower made his address. I felt like I was a part of history.

A woman at the front desk handed Alexa two room keys. We were more than ready to get settled in. Our room was definitely a reflection of the hotel. It was well furnished with polished oak wood.

After unpacking, neither Alexa nor I cared to take part in the meet and greet social they had scheduled. Instead, we decided to get some rest and attend the pajama party they had planned later on that evening.

I didn't even realize how hard and late I slept, because when I awoke, Alexa was nowhere to be found. I looked over at the radio-alarm clock on the end table and noticed the time was 10:10 P.M. I then felt serious hunger pangs coming on, and decided to get up and try to find something to eat. Before leaving the room, I took a shower and changed into some pajama pants, button-up pajama shirt, and slippers.

As I walked into the main lobby area, there were many people socializing, and as I moved closer to the ballroom, I could hear the hard bass of club music. To my relief, a food vendor was setup in the hallway. I did a magic trick of making my grilled chicken Caesar salad and lemon tea Snapple disappear.

As I looked around, I asked myself, *Where the hell is this girl? I knew I should've brought my cell phone with me.* I decided to walk over to the bar and order a drink. After all, open bar was included in this trip.

People swarmed the small bar area like bees on honey. You literally had to fight your way through the crowd. I may be small, but I can handle my own. And that's exactly what I did, shoving and pushing my way up front to a bartender. I felt bad for the two women serving drinks. They were working overtime, but were getting well tipped for their services.

"What can I get you, sweetie?" the bartender asked.

How can she maintain a smile after a night like this? I asked myself, but didn't expect an answer.

Just as I fixed my lips to place my order, I felt a shove at my back. *These people are getting a little beside themselves,* I thought.

"Y'all need to move back and stop acting like savages, okay!" I said defensively.

That's when the person who was causing this havoc made his way up front and said, "My bad, Ma," then dismissed me by turning away and saying to the bartender, "Yo, let me get a Thug Passion."

Oh, no! I am not his mother.

I thought about kicking him, but he was maybe three times my size, and I'm not talking about body fat. His muscular frame was well chiseled and couldn't have been any taller than five-nine. He wore a white wifebeater (tank top) with drawstring pajama pants and Nike running sneakers. His fair complexion was smooth, and his low haircut was perfectly trimmed with so many waves I almost got seasick. What scared me about this thug were the tattoos covering his arms. He also had one coming across his chest, back, and the word Roc on his neck.

Alexa didn't tell me there were going to be gang members on this trip, I thought. I just wanted to get my drink, go back to my room, and not come out until it was time to go home. Never again!

After receiving his drink, he pulled out a wad of money and left a generous tip, then pushed his way back through the crowd. I was glad he was gone, and managed to order an Apple Martini.

Just as I was making my way back to my room, I heard Alexa calling my name. She approached me, smiling and grinning.

"Girl, why didn't you tell me you were leaving?" I asked before she could say a word.

"I didn't want to wake you. Plus, Sincere had called me and I went up to his room. Girl, you have to see some of these people walking around in their pajamas."

I didn't really take much notice until Alexa mentioned it, and as I looked around, I noticed that some of these women had gotten this pajama party confused with a lingerie party. Many of them had no business wearing sheer or anything that revealed their bulging and stretch-marked stomachs. From the looks of it, some of them looked like they were wearing Spiderman costumes. Alexa's pajama set was as tasteful as mine, though.

"This guy is walking around wearing a robe with nothing on underneath, talking about he sleeps in the nude," Alexa managed to get out between laughs.

"Oh, no!" I said in an almost frightened voice. I didn't think any of this was funny.

"They're about to have a pajama and slipper contest. Let's go check it out."

"I'm okay."

"Come on, girl. Stop being so *bougie*."

I followed Alexa into the dark ballroom where the main party was being held. The dance floor was packed with people bumping, grinding, and jumping around to a serious mix of Hip Hop music as the DJ worked his butt off.

We stood off to the side of the dance floor, observing the scene. That's when Alexa pointed out Sincere speaking to the tattooed thug from the bar. Alexa leaned in and said loud enough so that I could hear, "There go Sincere and Roc."

I almost choked on my drink. I looked at Alexa as if she had grown two heads. "That's the guy you been trying to hook me up with?"

"What's wrong with him? He's cute, and he got mad money."

For a moment, I felt like Alexa was a complete stranger because she knew me much better than that. For one, I didn't need any help from her in the men department, and for two, there is no way I could see myself with a person who calls himself Roc and who has tattoos all over his body.

"You must've had one too many drinks tonight."

Alexa ignored my statement and said, "Come on, let's dance."

"Okay, let me go use the bathroom first."

"Hurry up back."

That was my excuse to escape to the sanctuary of my room.

Once I made it back, I finished off my drink, placed the empty glass on the end table, and got in bed. I couldn't help but laugh to myself at tonight's scene. I pray that tomorrow will be a much better day.

Saturday

I woke up just a little pass nine and noticed Alexa's bed was still made up. It was obvious she had stayed out, my guess, with Sincere. I felt like I was on this ski trip alone.

"Happy birthday," I said to myself in a low, groggy voice.

After taking a hot shower I pulled on a pair of blue jeans, a pullover black sweater, and a pair of black leather boots with a two-inch heel. I wanted to keep it simple and really throw it on for the evening party. I figured I'd start my day with a good breakfast and then inquire what was on today's itinerary.

The breakfast was setup buffet style. As I stood in line, I looked over the ballroom and saw no sign of Alexa. What alarmed me though was how so many women who came down for breakfast wore scarves on their heads and the pajamas they partied in last night.

How could they be so comfortable around men they hardly know? I thought.

As I sat indulging in pancakes, turkey sausage, orange juice, and a small fruit cup, I noticed Roc walking into the ballroom. We made eye contact, but didn't speak. As a matter of fact, he acted as if I was invisible. His rude behavior was really beginning to annoy me for some reason. Most men usually give an attractive woman a nod or something, but he passed by as if he was too good looking for a simple, "Hello."

After eating, I looked over the list of events planned for the day, and saw that there was a bus pulling out in five minutes for the shopping outlets. My demons quickly took over my body. Before I knew it, I was back in my room, putting on my coat, and double checking my wallet for credit cards. I decided to switch pocketbooks and carry my black leather handbag by Ralph Lauren, also described as The Ricky Bag. In a matter of minutes, I was rushing back downstairs to catch that bus.

It's been a long time since I've ran for a bus, I thought. But I felt it was worth it.

There were two buses preparing to leave for the shopping outlets, and I managed to get on one of them. Our tour guide informed us that this was a forty-five minute ride there and back, and that we would be able to shop for two hours.

That's more than enough time for me, I thought.

As I sat in the seat near the aisle, I laid my head back

and thought about how good it would've been to have a male companion accompany me on this trip. I almost envied Alexa, but I couldn't hate on her.

There are times when I would like to feel the comfort of a man. Sometimes I think about lowering my standards and settling down with the first guy that comes along. Those thoughts come even more knowing that my daughter will soon be off to college and I'll be alone. But then after I purchase something from Neiman Marcus, have a few glasses of wine, and take a hot bubble bath with candles burning while listening to the soulful sounds of Kem, I feel much better. I know plenty of women who married the first man that proposed to them, and they are now living with regrets.

The bus driver didn't know how much of a lifesaver he was by turning on the radio, because the smooth R&B distracted me from my lonely thoughts. I hummed along as Aretha Franklin sang, "Natural Woman."

Before long, we were at the shopping outlets. After being given a handful of coupons, I immediately checked the directory to see what this outlet had to offer. I then followed a trail leading to the Kenneth Cole clothing store.

I almost came on myself because I was in fashion heaven. I strolled through the store, touching the fabric of nearly every item in the women's department. There was a time when I wore things only "white kids" would wear, but that didn't go over too well in an all black school. Even though I had the body and long hair, I had no fashion sense, so I didn't fit in. But now, I receive heavy compliments for my taste in fashion. Not to mention, I have a serious shopping addiction.

God forgive me, but it feels so good to be able to shop solely for me and not my daughter, I thought.

As I was admiring a sweater, looking it over from front to back, placing it up against my body to see how it would look on me, a voice spoke from behind. "Get whatever you like and meet me at the register."

I turned to meet this stranger with the strange voice, and to my surprise, it was Roc.

"Excuse me? Yeah, okay," I said, laughing out loud. *That was cute,* I thought.

Roc smiled back, obviously admiring his own joke. He

must have been on the other bus. He was wearing a three quarter North Face snorkel zipped down, revealing the white thermal shirt he was wearing underneath. Hanging from his neck was a pair of dog tags with diamonds around the edges. His boot cut jeans fell perfectly over his Timberland boots.

"I didn't mean to startle you, but I felt the urge to come over and say something without coming off as a stalker."

"Okay," was all I could say, still smiling. He wasn't bad looking, just not my type.

"May I ask your name?"

I figured it was best to be polite. I didn't want to offend him. There's no telling what he was capable of. Besides, he kept following me as I tried to shop. "Chanel."

Roc held in his laughter. "Are you serious?"

"Is pig pork?"

"You're funny. Your parents actually named you Chanel?"

"Something's wrong with that?"

"Not at all."

"What's your name?" I already knew, but he didn't know that.

"Roc."

Now it was my turn to laugh. "I know that's not what your mother named you?"

"No, it's not."

He didn't fill in the blank, so I took it as though he didn't want me to know his real name. He probably has warrants and is in a gang. *Just let it go, girl,* I told myself.

"What's so funny?" he asked.

"Nothing, I'm just thinking about something."

Maybe Alexa was right about him. He doesn't seem so bad after all. I just hoped he didn't take this as an open invitation to harass me the entire weekend. I felt I had better end this little conversation.

"Okay, Roc, it was nice meeting you, but I have to use this time wisely."

"Okay, Chanel. I'll be seeing you around."

It wasn't what he said; it's how he said it, with a hidden seductive tone. Roc strolled away and walked over into the men's department where two of his friends were watching. I felt it was best to find another store to browse in.

During my ride back to the hotel, I couldn't help to admire Roc's suaveness and bold attitude. He was a bit cocky, but every woman likes that in a man.

Girl, I know you're not thinking about that man, my inner voice asked as I looked out the window, trying to distract my thoughts. As I smiled and shook my head at my own question, Marvin Gaye's "Let's Get It On" hit the airwaves. His soothing voice calmed me and took me into relaxation mode. I didn't even feel myself dozing off until someone nudged me.

"Hey, baby, we here," the older woman next to me said with a smile. "You were out like a light."

I smiled back. "Yes, I was. Thank you."

After getting off the bus, I headed back to my room with bags in hand, feeling good about my light shopping spree. Stepping inside the room, to my surprise, Alexa was there putting on her coat.

"I should've known your ass was out shopping," she said.

"You know me."

Then, Alexa broke out and started singing "Happy Birthday," Stevie Wonder's version.

"Girl, please," I said with a cheesy smile, while placing my bags on the bed. "Where you on your way to?"

"*We* are about to go skating."

"Okay, let me use the bathroom first."

After freshening up a bit, I wanted to try on my new clothes and give Alexa a fashion show, but she wasn't interested. She insisted that I go roller skating with her. While on the bus, it dawned on me that this was the first time since coming to PA Alexa and I were actually spending time together.

"Are you enjoying yourself yet?" Alexa asked.

"I'm doing fine."

"Well, we still have to go to the swimming pool party. That's going to be off the hook. And then we have to go to the party later on tonight. You haven't seen anything you like yet?"

"I'm not paying these guys no mind. I'm just enjoying my time away from home, work, and Raven."

We both had to laugh at that.

"Girl, it's your birthday. Loosen up a bit. Enjoy life."

"I am. What's up with Sincere?" I asked, taking the conversation off of me.

"Girl, I almost had to go upside his head last night."

"What happened?"

"He leaves out the room to go get some ice. Five minutes go by, and I'm like, 'It don't take that damn long to get no ice.' I leave and go looking for him; he's all up in some bitch's face. I almost lost it."

"Girl, you live for drama."

"Whatever. He drives me crazy sometimes."

I was only off the hook for a short while. Alexa wouldn't let up. She tried her best to convince me to "hook up" with someone while away for the weekend, but I couldn't just get down with a guy I didn't know. I at least have to have some attraction for him, and I didn't see anyone that caught my attention that I would even consider sleeping with.

"You need to stop being so picky," Alexa said.

"No, I don't. I'ma be all right. I brought my bullet in case of an emergency."

"Girl, all this dick running around here…" Alexa said, cutting her sentence short as if that was enough said.

All I could do was laugh and shake my head, because I

could always count on Alexa to keep it real and speak her mind. But I just couldn't get down with her logic.

I wanted to give the bus driver a hug and kiss when he announced we were at our destination, because he gave me an escape from Alexa's conversation.

It's been awhile since I've put on a pair of roller skates. Alexa is much more experienced, so I had to follow her lead. We carried on like teenagers, falling all over the place, nearly causing a pile up. Many advanced skaters shook their heads in disgust because we were messing up their groove, but we didn't care.

Time does fly by when you're having fun, because before we knew it, we were back on the bus heading toward the hotel. To get off my sex life, I kept Alexa entertained by reliving the events at the skating rink.

Once back at the hotel, we ate dinner and then decided to take a nap. After about two hours of deep sleep, I awoke and smiled at the sight of Alexa still in her bed. My girl really spent the day with me for my birthday. After awakening her, we both decided it was time to change and get dressed for the swimming pool party. I put on a two-piece bathing suit and tied a wrap around my waist, letting it fall down to my thighs, leaving something for the imagination. I figured I'd wear a pair of flip flops, displaying my pedicure, just in case I decided to get in the water. Alexa, on the other hand, threw on a bikini bathing suit with a sheer wrap tied around her waist and coming down to her thighs, with a pair of three-inch pumps.

"Girl, where the hell you think you're going with those pumps on?" I had to ask.

"I'ma get in the bathing suit contest."

All I could do was shake my head. We stepped into a section of the hotel that housed a tropical indoor pool and Jacuzzi plaza. The DJ was already in a serious mix of R&B music, and the party had been going on for an hour. Mostly everyone came dressed for the occasion. Still, there were some brothas in jeans and boots.

They probably are doing us all a favor, I thought.

I liked how the women were dressed accordingly. Those who didn't have the body didn't reveal it, and those who did were one string away from being nude. The men, on the other hand, well, it's a shame how they can get away with damn near any and everything. Many of them were one burger away from being obese, but that didn't stop them from showing off their bodies.

A group of people were in a game of musical chairs. It was funny seeing them fight half-naked for a vacant seat every time the music stopped. At the end of the game, there was only one person standing. She managed to pull the chair from up under the guy as he tried to take a seat. Everyone broke out in a roaring laughter as she sat down, turned to the brotha on the ground, and said with serious attitude, "Too slow, *biatch*!"

Then, the DJ announced the bathing suit contest.

Alexa turned to me and said, "You getting in?"

"Girl, you know better than that."

Although my body was in pretty decent shape, I still didn't see the need to put it on display. After having my daughter, I became a little self-conscious about my physical appearance. I don't care how good a woman looks; after giving birth, she never sees herself the same.

The DJ first announced the men. There were about twenty of them lined up. As they stepped out, one by one, they received applauds, dog barks, and cat calls from the spectators

as the hype man instigated the scene. It was obvious that many
of them lived in the gym. Everyone laughed when the six feet,
reed thin model walked out. Following him was the short, plump
model with a serious pot belly.

Then, all eyes fell on Roc when he came out. Alexa gave
me a nudge and a devilish grin. He wore a pair of swimming
trunks and Timberland boots, his dog tags hanging from his neck.
He strolled around so everyone could get a good look. He never
broke a smile, looking serious and mysterious as if he was up to
something or looking for someone. His tattoos stretched across
the upper part of his oiled body. He walked over to where Alexa
and me were standing, and held his gaze on me for more than a
minute. I had to use every bit of strength I had in my body to
keep from crumbling.

I'm glad I brought my toy, I thought.

Roc and all these attractive bodies had my hormones
doing cartwheels and somersaults. After the males had done
their thing, it was time for the audience to announce the winner.
The hype man held a hand over each competitor, and whoever
received the loudest cheers won. Needless to say, the six feet, reed

thin model won $100 for his boldness.

Then, the women lined up, all thirty of them, and took the spotlight. As each of them strutted their elegant bodies across the floor, the men lost it. Even the women on the sideline had to give them their props. Of course, some looked better than others, but overall, they all looked good. Short, tall, dark, or light, whatever you desired was provided.

Alexa walked out and everyone loved her. When she loosened the wrap from around her waist and revealed all that she had to offer, everyone went wild. The fellas were like, "Damn!" and the women were like, "Okay!" I just knew my girl had this one in the bag.

That's when the DJ brought everyone's attention to the next model waiting to come out. She stood in a stance like a runway model, with her hands on her small waist. There was a glow about this woman. Her caramel complexion and big, light brown eyes almost had *me* hypnotized. The DJ mixed the music from Hip Hop to club, and on cue, she stepped out in long strides, full of confidence. Her five-nine frame was built like a dancer. The men could not control themselves. She even made some of the women cover in shame. Her two-piece swimsuit was

nothing but two strings. She turned the party out by wiggling her

ass and making her cheeks clap.

"Yeah, Jazzy! Do that shit!" someone yelled out. There

were a group of cheerleaders on the side encouraging her erotic

dance.

"This trifling bitch," Alexa said more to herself than to

anyone in particular. It was no longer a bathing suit contest.

It was all about body parts. We both knew who would be the

winner after this performance.

After the swimming pool party, we went back to our

rooms with our heads hung low in defeat. I tried to cheer Alexa

up by trying to make my butt clap, imitating the erotic dancer.

Alexa cracked up big time because we both know there wasn't

enough back there for that.

Once inside the room, we laughed and talked some more

about the day's events, and then decided to get dressed for the

evening party.

I wanted to stay within the season and wear something

elegant and classy. After giving it some thought, I decided to wear an outfit I purchased from Banana Republic and a pair of boots from Nine West. Which is my black leather, high rise boots with a square flat heel, a pair of grey cropped pants, a white ruffled shirt that I tucked in my pants, and a black blazer. Alexa threw on a black fitted dress that hit at her thighs. It had an open back with an open front, revealing her flat stomach and covering her breast like a bra. On her feet was a pair of black pointy toe boots with a three-inch heel.

To add to my outfit, I put on my accessories: diamond studded earrings, Gucci watch, and diamond ring. Alexa just wore some diamond studded earrings and a belly ring. We felt fabulous and looked glamorous.

There was a red carpet leading to the entrance of the ballroom and a photographer taking pictures of everyone walking down the runway. Alexa and me stopped over at the picture booth and took a few photos. We then walked over to the bar and ordered Apple Martinis before stepping into the ballroom. There were eyes on us from men and women.

We did a little mixing and mingling with familiar faces. The DJ was playing a serious mix of club music. The hard bass was communicating with my soul. As I finished my drink, I placed the empty glass down on a table and turned to Alexa. "This is my song. I'm going on the dance floor."

"Do your thing, girl. I'll be out there in a minute."

Linda Clifford's "Runaway Love" moved my spirit and guided my body across the dance floor. I added a little dip to my two-step routine. When the group Ecstasy, Pain, and Passion's "Touch and Go" came on, I almost lost it. A well of emotions suddenly built up inside of me. I was so lost in the words and rhythm of the song that I could barely hear the DJ shouting me out for my birthday. I'm sure that was Alexa's doing.

I picked up my pace a little and started coming up with dance moves all on my own, as Lolita Holloway's "Hit and Run" filled the room. As I was letting the soulful sounds wash over me, I felt a presence from behind. I didn't really want to dance with anyone, and hated when guys take it upon themselves to get all up on me when I'm dancing. My first thought was to stop and walk away, but my feet wouldn't allow it, so I turned around to meet the intruder.

To my surprise, it was Roc. He looked every bit of

debonair in a pair of blue jeans, white button-up shirt, and beige blazer. On his feet were brown loafers.

I smiled as he tried to outdo me on the dance floor. He jumped up, spun around, and dipped down to the floor. Then, he came back up, slid to the left, and back to the right. He had some serious footwork.

When Womack and Womack's "Baby, I'm Scared of You" came on, Roc slipped into a world of his own. I wanted to say *You go, boy,* but he didn't need any encouragement from me. He was definitely turning up the heat, as I used the photo I took as a fan. He started lip-synching the male's version, adding a little dramatization to it as if he wrote the lyrics. What I really admired was that he didn't try to grope me or disrespect my space, and I gave him points for that.

The DJ then ended my happy moment by switching to Fifty Cent's "Candy Shop." This was my cue to make my exit. I thanked Roc and walked off.

On the side, I watched as he gathered with others on the dance floor. Alexa and Sincere had even joined in, singing along and throwing their fists in the air.

I shook my head and laughed out loud. *That girl knows she's gangsta.*

People started jumping up and down, screaming out the song, and bouncing hard to the beat, as if they wrote and produced the track.

Roc blended in with the crowd. He really started getting into the music. He even unbuttoned his shirt, revealing the white wifebeater underneath. The veins started coming out of his neck. He was really feeling the G-Unit and Fifty Cent mix. I imagined him using that same force in bed, going in and out of me. The thought made me wet. I had to leave the ballroom to get some air and something to drink.

To my surprise, the bar in the lobby area wasn't crowded. I waited for the person in front of me to receive their drink. Just as I was about to place my order, someone from behind said, "Let me get a Thug Passion."

I turned to my right, and Roc had a big, cheesy smile on his face.

"You know, that's the second time you cut in front of me."

"I'm just messing with you."

"Yeah, okay. What's up with you and this drink? What is it anyway?"

"Hennessey and Alize. It's safe enough for a woman, but made for a man."

I had to smile at his sense of humor. "Whatever. You know what, let me get a Thug Passion, as well," I said to the bartender.

Roc smiled. "You were doing your thing in there."

"You had a little footwork yourself."

"I do what I can do." He caught me off guard when he said, "I like your hairstyle. You have beautiful, healthy hair. It has mad body and bounce. What's your secret?"

"Thanks," I said, touching a curl. "I use a pretty good shampoo and conditioner."

"I see. Let me check out your pic," Roc said, gesturing to the picture of me and Alexa I placed on the bar.

I handed it to him. He nodded and said, "Nice," then gave the picture back to me.

After receiving our drinks and tipping the bartender, we decided to sit in the lobby area.

"You come on these trips often?" I asked, placing the picture in my lap.

"Naw, this is actually my first time. My man Sincere put me onto this."

"Yeah, that's pretty much my case. Alexa convinced me to come for my birthday."

"Happy birthday. I thought I heard the DJ giving you a shout out."

"Yeah, thanks. You seem to know a little about hair. You must have an older sister, or is that your pickup line?"

Roc smiled. "A little of both. Yeah, I have an older sister, but she didn't teach me anything about hair. As a matter of fact, I be schoolin' her. Naw, I'm a licensed barber and own a unisex salon on Chancellor in Newark. I've been in the business for about ten years."

Roc had just received an approval of acceptance. I was obviously judging the book by its cover.

He threw me off when he asked, "By the way, how old are you?"

"Nineteen," I replied with a serious expression.

Roc smiled, obviously knowing I was far from nineteen. He held up his cup and said, "I'll drink to that. Bottoms up, baby." We tapped cups, and then guzzled down our drinks. The bittersweet taste stung the back of my throat, but I wanted to show Roc that I could hang with the big boys. I didn't bring the cup down until I swallowed every drop.

"Damn! Okay, Killa. You ready for round two?"

"Keep it comin'," I said with a smile.

As Roc stepped away to get refills, I started to see him with a new vision. He didn't seem as hardcore as I had made him out to be. He actually had style, class, and a sense of humor. If he was putting up a front, he should change his profession to acting.

When he returned with our drinks, I swallowed the second Thug Passion down in two gulps. After about ten minutes, the alcohol came down on me hard and heavy. My head started to spin and my body started to float. My body temperature rose, and I had to use my picture again as a fan. I tried to stand, but found myself stumbling, falling off balance. I definitely had one too many.

"Whoa! I think I had too much to drink," I said, and then

laughed out loud.

Roc laughed, but not as hard as me. He had to help me stand.

"You sure you gonna be all right?"

"I'm aw-ight? You aw-ight?" I laughed again at my boldness. The spirits of the alcohol was definitely working on my mental. "I need to lie down."

"Come on; let me walk you to your room."

Not a bad idea, I thought.

We walked down the corridor…well, I stumbled and he pretty much led the way. After several steps, I was able to gather my composure and walk without Roc's support. There were others lounging around—guys trying to lay their Mack down on the women who were either drunk or available for the weekend.

Two guys were passing by. One of them said, "I see your work, Roc."

"And I see yours, *bitch*." The alcohol had me thinking I could say and do whatever I wanted. Roc must've understood my state of mind, because he, along with a few others, laughed. The male just brushed my smart comment off and kept walking, trying to hold on to his pride.

We finally made it to my room. It seemed like it took forever. My body felt like it was being pulled down by quicksand. I didn't have to ask, because once I opened the door, Roc let himself in.

I walked deeper into the room and turned on a lamp. The dim lighting was satisfying for my eyes. I then tossed the picture on the table, took off my blazer, placed it on a chair, cracked a window, sat on the edge of the bed, and then fell on my back. I looked up and noticed Roc had hung up his blazer and shirt. I couldn't help to wonder how long he had planned to stay, but the sight of his muscular frame standing in front of me wearing a wifebeater and jeans was very pleasing.

"Can you please take off my boots?" I managed to ask.

Roc kneeled down, unzipped my boots, and took them off, one at a time, along with my socks. He then placed them to the side and asked, "Do you need help taking anything else off?"

I smiled.

He was way too kind, but I felt I could manage on my own. My body felt like it was on fire, and the only way I could cool off was to rid myself of my clothes. I found enough strength to unfasten my pants and pull them off all by myself. My shirt, however, wasn't so simple. I had to sit up. Roc noticed me struggling with my buttons and came to my rescue.

I lay there in a haze, wearing black lace panties with a matching bra. The cool air coming through the window, hitting against my skin, was very inviting. I then felt wet kisses on my left leg. I looked up and noticed Roc was naked.

His tongue traveled up to my thighs while pulling off my panties. As if he needed some guidance, I spread my legs and used my fingers to lead him in the direction where I wanted to be licked. We had known each other for hardly a day and this man had his face buried in my crotch, as if we were longtime lovers. But I welcomed the pleasure, and to show my gratitude, I grabbed Roc by the back of his head, gyrated my hips, and pulled him deeper into me.

"That's it, baby. Suck it."

It was a small battle, but he managed to break free from my vice grip and come up for air.

I moved further up on the bed. As he started to climb

on me, I managed to reach down to make sure he was wearing some protection. He was well protected, but I expected him to be packing a little more down there. He wasn't the biggest or the smallest I had to work with.

His penis departed my flesh and traveled through my walls. It was satisfying. He moved in and out of me a little faster than I liked for him to, but I was enjoying myself. I closed my eyes and concentrated on our body language.

"You like that, baby?" he asked, pounding away.

I wanted to say, *Shut up, I'm trying to concentrate.* But instead, I said, "Yeah, baby, keep doing it like that."

After a few minutes, Roc began to grunt and moan loudly. His body stiffened. I didn't know what was going on at first, but then it became obvious. Roc had exploded into small pebbles. My mind screamed, *What the fuck was that!*

It was like the needle that scratched the record at the height of a banging club. No, it was more like fingernails clawing down a chalkboard.

"Aw, shit," was his weak response as he pulled out.

"What happened?" It was a stupid question, but it was the

first thing that came out of my mouth.

"Yo, your shit is too wet. Damn, you got some good pussy."

"Okay." *Tell me something I don't know,* I thought. "Where you going?"

"Hold up. I gotta take this condom off."

Roc stepped into the bathroom. My high was coming to a low, and I wanted to curse his ass out. He definitely had to finish what he started. After hearing the toilet flush, Roc walked back over to the bed and lay down beside me.

"I hope you got another condom?"

"Yeah, but I'ma need some help getting hard again."

I had about enough of fun and games for one night. I seriously needed to release with or without his help. I know he probably was expecting me to go down on him, but I had other plans.

With a seductive smile, I said, "Lay on your stomach. I want to kiss your back."

Without any hesitation, Roc stretched across the bed, resting his head on his arms. Painted in black, down the full length of his back, was a cross.

I started with soft, wet kisses on his neck, and then rolled my tongue down the spine of his back, stopping just at the crack. I squeezed his tight, round ass, smacked it, massaged both cheeks, and then climbed on top.

"Damn, baby, you got a nice body," I commented.

"It's all yours."

"Oh, really?"

"That's if you want it."

I didn't even bother to answer that one. I was too focused on meeting my needs. With my clit pressed against his body, I began to ride him, slowly.

"Damn, baby, I wanna ride your ass." I then picked up my pace and started to pump harder. Roc fell into rhythm and moved his body with mine.

"Yes, baby, give me this fat ass," I said as I reached behind and grabbed a cheek.

He lifted himself off the bed a little in a pushup position, and I reached around to jerk him. I then used my other hand to squeeze his bootie, and then slid my fingers between the crack.

I massaged the middle, and the moistness made it easy for my finger to slide in. His body jerked a little, but he didn't stop throwing his ass up at me. Most men allow their egos to get in the way when it came to this type of affection, but Roc was down for whatever.

"Yeah, baby, come on. Give it to me," I encouraged.

I then let go of his penis, and with forcefulness, I grabbed the back of his neck and rode his ass even harder.

"You my bitch? Huh? You my bitch?" I asked, more like demanded.

Either he was just going along with it or just as tipsy as me, because he said in a low voice, "Yeah, I'm your bitch."

This caused my clitoris to tingle.

"Oh, yeah, baby, here it come!" Then, a flood of emotions came pouring down until there was a sticky puddle running off the high end of his ass to his lower back. I rolled off this high horse and fell onto my back. Roc got up, and I believe he went into the bathroom.

Moments later, I heard Roc say, "My turn now."

With blurred vision, I noticed Roc putting on another

condom and then climbing up on the bed. He went in and out of me faster than a Road Runner, and just like the first time, he came again.

Poor, poor Roc, I thought. *If only he could learn to take his time, he would be okay.*

He then pulled out, but this time, I managed to curl up under the covers. I heard Roc mumbling something about he had to go, and then after about a minute or two, I heard the door close. Satisfied, I drifted off into a deep sleep.

Sunday

I slept the entire morning. The time on the radio-alarm clock displayed 3:30 P.M. When I did sit up, I immediately grabbed my head with both hands to keep it from falling off my shoulders.

What in the hell was in those drinks, I thought.

Throat dry and feeling dehydrated, I pulled the covers off me. My mouth fell open when I realized I had nothing on except my bra.

What in the hell did I do last night, my mind screamed.

As I stepped out of bed, I saw a condom wrapper on the floor, picked it up, and then out of reaction, touched between my legs. I was moist and smelt like sex. I tried to pull myself together and collect my thoughts from last night. The entire evening seemed to be a big blur. I looked over at Alexa's bed and it hadn't been touched. She must've stayed with Sincere.

I headed for the bathroom to bathe and dispose of any evidence that sex was performed in my room.

I managed to make it down in time for dinner and catch the comedy show, the last event before checking out of our rooms. After piling my plate with baked chicken, a garden salad, and mashed potatoes, I scanned the ballroom and noticed Alexa sitting with Roc, Sincere, and a few others I didn't quite know. Too embarrassed to join them, I decided to sit at a table with a small group of strangers. As I sat, they acknowledged me with friendly gestures, but didn't really pay me any mind.

As each of the three comedians performed, all I could think about was last night. I kept glancing over at Alexa, Sincere, and Roc, and couldn't help to wonder if my name was mentioned in their conversation. I wondered if Roc was the type of man who gossiped to his friends about his sex life.

Alexa would never let me forget this if she found out, I thought.

I started to have regrets of ever stepping foot on the bus that brought me to Gettysburg.

What's done is done, I tried to convince myself. I was grateful for the West Coast comedian onstage, because he did distract my thoughts for a moment.

After the comedy show, the DJ announced last call for alcohol and opened the floor for a final hour of partying before we had to load the buses. I decided to go back to my room and pack.

As I stepped out of the ballroom, I felt a light tug at my arm. I immediately became defensive because I thought it was some knucklehead trying to grab my attention for some lame game. Instead, it was Roc.

"Where you going so fast?" he asked.

I should've asked you that question last night, I thought. Instead, I said, "To my room to pack."

"You need some help?"

"I'm okay. Thanks."

"I'd love to take you out some time, get to know you a little better. You think that's possible?"

"I don't think so. Look, Roc, last night—"

"Was between us. Here," he said, pulling something out of his back pocket. "Take a flyer. Check me out the next time you decide to get your hair done."

"Oh, okay. I'll do that."

I looked over the flyer, smiled, and then walked away. As I moved down the corridor, I could feel Roc's eyes on my back. As I turned a corner, I managed to look over my shoulder, and my guess was right. He was still there, watching me.

I quickly packed and decided to wait in the lobby. I figured Alexa could play catch up. I was more than ready to get back home.

"Girl, where you been?" Alexa asked when she finally caught up with me in the lobby. We both had our luggage and ready to board the bus. "I was looking all over for you. And why are you not answering your phone?"

"Okay, *Mommy*, which question should I answer first?"

"Whatever," Alexa replied, laughing off my sarcasm. "Watch my bags while I turn my key in."

As Alexa walked over to the front desk, I tried to detect any hint of her knowing about Roc and me, but she didn't give away any sign. Moments later, someone announced we could board the buses, and I was one of the first to jump up.

"So did you have fun?" Alexa asked once we got settled. She sat near the aisle.

"It was okay. I'm just ready to get home so I can get some rest. I wish I didn't have to work tomorrow."

"Girl, don't even talk about work."

Once again, Smooth demanded our attention.

"A'ight, y'all, listen up," he spoke into the microphone. "For those of you who are too drunk to remember, my name is Smooth, your bus captain. Now, y'all know the rules, so I won't even repeat 'em. I just wanted to thank y'all for supporting another nHouse Entertainment event. I'll be coming around to collect a donation for our bus driver, who got us down here safe and will make sure we make it back to our families and loved ones in one piece. I'ma also pass around some flyers for our crab fest this summer. If you enjoyed yourselves this weekend, you'll even have more fun in D.C."

Alexa leaned in and said, "We should go to their crab fest. I know Roc and Sincere are gonna go."

I gave Alexa a weak smile.

"For all you newcomers," Roc continued, picking up where Smooth left off, "if you see me on the street, you do not know me from this ski trip. As a matter of fact, don't even mention anything about a ski trip." Those who knew where Roc was going with this laughed.

Smooth cut back in. "As I said on the way coming down, what goes on in PA," and again, in unison, nearly every person on the bus said, "stays in PA," and then broke out in laughter.

Smooth said, "Now that's what I'm talkin' 'bout."

Alexa turned to me and smiled. I tried to read between the lines.

"What?" I asked.

"Nothing." She smiled even harder, and then snuggled up in the chair and closed her eyes.

I think I had enough of weekend getaways with Alexa, I thought as we gave the Eisenhower Resort and Gettysburg our farewell.

Payback After Dark

Some say revenge is best served cold, but I believe it is best served hot and in public. I came to this epiphany because of a fake ass bitch that took my kindness for weakness and tried to play me for a sucker. I'm not saying I'm all that, but I'm not to be taken for a joke. I mean like, don't pee on my head and tell me it's rain.

Rickey Sanders had no reason to play me like that, especially when all I tried to do was be her friend.

We hung out one night, did some serious club hopping, came back to my place, and crashed. I thought she was cool people at the time. She was a fly dresser and flirted like flirting was going out of style. We didn't have to buy one drink that night.

During that summer of 2007, I was keeping my lesbian status on the down low, so I didn't bring her back to my place to jump her bones. I really liked her, enjoyed her company. I never forced any chick to get down with me. As a matter of fact, it was her idea to come back to my place.

I didn't expect anything. I really didn't, but we had been drinking and I couldn't see her driving home until she got her head straight. I even made a little bed for her on my living room couch. After she took a nice hot shower, I told her to sleep well and that I'd fix her breakfast in the morning. I even let her wear one of my nightgowns.

I took my shower, and when I came out of the bathroom, the light was out in the living room. I figured that Ricky was asleep.

I went into my bedroom, peeled off my towel, and let it drop to the hardwood floor. The only light was coming from the open blinds.

"You got a nice, tight body," Rickey voiced from behind me.

I looked over my bare shoulder and found my guest standing in the doorway.

"A nice, tight dancer's body," Rickey went on, like I had asked her to come into my private space to check me out.

As a dancer with the Marcus Salley Dance Company, I was used to folks looking at me, checking out the long lines of my body. I didn't know where Rickey was going with the compliments, but she acted like she couldn't keep her eyes off me.

"You mind if I turn on the lights?" she asked.

"Knock yourself out," I told her, trying to appear nonchalant, like I didn't give a fuck. But my heart was pounding like a drum in my chest, and there was sweat between my breasts.

Rickey stared at me like she was fascinated by my dark nipples and shaved coochie. I thought about spreading it for her, but I didn't want to scare the chick away. Like I said, I hadn't thought about getting down with Rickey Sanders, but with her standing there in the little nightie I had given her, she was making me mad horny.

I climbed into my bed and pulled a single white sheet up, tucking it under my arms. I didn't know what Rickey had in mind, so I let her make the first move. I had told her that I'd had sexual experiences with women, but I never told her that women were all I had dealt with; dick was not on my menu.

That night at the club, I had let many men buy me

drinks, but I didn't encourage them to even think they were getting anything more than a wink and a smile from me, Angela King. However, with Rickey looking at me like she wanted to eat me up, I had to admit that I was down for anything.

"I've never considered myself a lesbian," Rickey told me. "But looking at you, Angela, and with you smiling at me, it's a real turn on, girl. I don't think I will ever give up men, but getting down with you would be pure pleasure."

I watched Rickey as she pushed down the thin straps of the nightie. Her shoulders were nice and round, and her skin was caramel colored. Then, she walked over and stood by the side of the bed.

I didn't say a word when she began tugging at my sheet. She didn't stop tugging until I was sitting up in my bed naked. Rickey then crawled in between my legs. She pushed my legs apart and pressed her face into my coochie. I threw my legs over her shoulders, and she cupped my butt with her hands. She had me squirming all over that bed, with her tongue all up inside me. She even licked my anus, causing me to almost come like that.

"I've been waiting to do that for a long time," Rickey told

me, as she sat back on her heels.

By that time, the nightie was a thick rope around her waist. Her belly was flat and smooth, and I just had to lick and suck her navel. I pushed the nightie down her hips. While she kneeled on both knees, I pushed her back so that she was flat on the bed. With her thighs opened wide, I went down on her neatly trimmed coochie.

Rickey pulled away from me because she didn't want to reach her climax from me eating her out. She told me to get on top and rub my clit against her clit; we came together like that.

We had a great time that night.

However, when I ran into her a few weeks later, Rickey acted like she didn't know me, like she had never tasted my coochie. She was at the club with some guys. I spoke to her, but she didn't say anything. She looked through me like I was a ghost. Made me think that just maybe I had dreamt we had been together in my bed.

I figured I'd let it slide, until I was given a flyer on the streets. This was a few months after my sexual encounter with that bitch.

"You must check out this hot singer," the guy told me. "She puts on a hot show."

It was billed as Adult Hip Hop Entertainment, and featured a new artist who called herself "Cassandra"; I knew her as Rickey Sanders.

"Two faced bitch!" I said as I walked down the street with the flyer that announced the show at The New Club House.

When I met her, Rickey had long, frosted hair. I think she was trying to be a black Farrah Fawcett, that Charlie's Angels TV chick from back in the day. Rickey was a little spacey, but we did hit if off. I had never heard her sing, but she always struck me as the kind of chick that could do anything she put her mind to.

I stared at the Cassandra/Rickey mug shot. A hood covered her head, and it was obvious that she had cut all her hair off. Her show was called "A Tribute to Lady Clarissa," the underground sensation rumored to give a hot show.

Because I was not sure if I really wanted to see that bitch in performance, I got to the club super late and missed the first show. The buzz in the club was that the second show, the late show, was the show to see. That's when Cassandra would present "the raw shit," according to a chick I was next to in the standing room only crowd.

"Was she any good?" I asked the chick.

"Not bad, not bad at all. And her look is all that. Not too many women can rock that baldhead style and still look femme. I have to admit, Cassandra pulled it off in grand style."

"And you say this second show is going to be even hotter?"

"It's gonna be like a Lady Clarissa show."

"I've never seen a Lady Clarissa show."

"Well, hold on to your socks 'cause it's gonna be all that. I'm staying to see Cassandra do her thing; it's going to be off the hook. I got to see it. I don't want anybody telling me what I missed."

That's when the announcement came over the loudspeaker system. "Ladies and gentlemen, The New Club House will be presenting an adults only show. If you can't deal with true adult entertainment, or if you're an undercover cop, it's time for you to go. Cassandra is about to let it all hang out in the style of Lady Clarissa. If the sight of a hot diva doing her thing offends you, this is the time for you to get your hat and leave. To ensure the intimacy of this event, the doors of The New Club House will be locked. No one will be allowed in or out while we bring you this special show."

WJDM's Bobby Butler was the MC. "I want to thank you for hanging out for this very special show," he said to the audience. He was smiling from ear to ear, showing straight white teeth, and dressed in a white shirt, a bow tie he tied himself, and a midnight blue tux. He looked good, standing up there in front of the band, his radio trained voice booming loud.

"Earlier this evening, Cassandra sang her soon-to-be released hit from Are You Ready Records, a tune entitled 'Way Out'," Bobby Butler went on. "But the next set will feature songs you won't hear on the radio. As a matter of fact, you won't hear any of these songs unless you see this exciting newcomer all the way live and after dark. This is the show everybody will be talking about, a show that makes legends."

That was when the band began to play.

"Ladies and Gentlemen, I give you Are You Ready Records' recording artist... Cassandra!"

Rickey came out in a long, hooded black robe, and the audience went wild, clapping and stomping like this "Cassandra" was the second coming of Lady Clarissa. With a shake of her head, the hood fell to her shoulders. Her round head was clean shaven.

"The day I shaved my head, I felt truly free," Rickey/Cassandra told us, moving on the stage in her bare feet. She wasn't dancing, but her movements were in sync with the hard driving music that bubbled up from behind her.

I wondered how she would feel if she knew I was in the audience.

"At that point, I knew I had to go my own way," Cassandra told us. "Follow my own path. With my music, my songs, I knew I had to do me. But that's not the only thing I've changed. This first song talks about another big change in my life. I call it 'About Your Girl'. There's a kiddy version on the new CD, *Freestyle Supreme*. This here tonight is the raw shit."

That was when she pulled the mike off its stand. Cassandra sang:

"I know you saw me / Coming out of the ladies' room, /

Looking sleek and oh so smooth. / I tried to ignore you, / But you make me say, 'Hi,' / Showed me that you were / Just like the other guys. / Can't believe it's not all about you. / Listen while I school you. / It isn't about you / When I give my hips a twirl. / It isn't about you, brother. / It's about your girl."

Some of the crowd, mostly women, laughed when they realized where Cassandra was going with her song. She continued to sing:

"I'm not hating 'cause / I know that you play. / To all the girls you're / Just another lay. / All excited by the way / You put it down. / What about your girl / When you're not around? / It ain't about you / When I give my hips a twirl. / It ain't about you, boy. / It's about your girl."

I looked around the club and saw that the crowd was really into Cassandra's music, nodding their heads, feeling this scandalous display. The sexy singer sang:

"It ain't about you, / But you can't believe that. / Just like that dog that couldn't catch that cat. / You ain't

shit and that's where it's at. / She's no longer under your thumb. / She looks at you and sees a bum. / Laughing like you got game. / Player getting played and it's a damn shame. / And it ain't about you / When I give these hips a twirl / It ain't about you, sucker. / It's about your girl."

Cassandra danced and sang as she moved along the stage. At any minute, I expected her to break into a full out boogie because the music was just that hot. She sang:

"When we had a meeting in the ladies' room, / It wasn't about you / Or the sorry things you do. / Your girl is just tired of you / In a major way. / Remember every dog has his day. / I gave her a shoulder to cry on and a place to rest her mind / To get over the hurt caused by your sorry behind. / In the bedroom, I'm gonna seal the deal. / You were okay, but you wasn't real. / She said you were good, but that's all right. / The love I'll put on her will be out of sight. / It ain't about you. / It's about your girl."

I found myself patting my thighs and swaying to the

music as Cassandra put it down heavy. She sang:

> *"Now she's coming to me trembling with need. / I have*
>
> *to give you credit, you planted the seed. / But the seed*
>
> *you planted was so small, / She won't even remember*
>
> *your name when you call. / I had to go in deep to erase*
>
> *her fear. / Her sweet moans were music in my ear. /*
>
> *Now she's rocking hot and heavy on my jock. / She says*
>
> *she can't stand your little cock. / And it ain't about you*
>
> *when I put it down. / It ain't about you / 'Cause you're*
>
> *no longer around."*

The applause was scattered, but genuine, even from some of the men. It was clear what Cassandra was saying: she had no use for men anymore. I was in complete agreement. Some men felt that they could never be replaced. I laughed and clapped along with the crowd, because I knew how expendable men really were.

"I'm sorry, guys," Cassandra said from the stage as she ran her hands up and down her robed body. "All this is for the girls and for one very special lady tonight. I missed my idol's Lady Clarissa's performance at this very club last week. But I heard that Lady C threw down hard. I'm gonna throw it down even harder. You gonna remember Cassandra. I plan to make this a performance you will never forget."

The singer smiled at the crowd as she pulled the zipper down on her robe, exposing the fact that she wore no bra. There was deep cleavage between her breasts as she continued to pull the zipper down to expose her flat belly. "Lady C showed you all her stuff, allowing you to look deep inside her funky imagination."

That was when the singer moved her hips in tight circles as the band played loud behind her. "I heard what she did," Cassandra said as she pulled up the bottom of her robe, pushing the garment up and over her head. Once naked, she said, "All smooth. I got a body wax all over my body."

The crowd exploded with applause, enthusiastically accepting her.

I shook my head, amazed, wondering where Rickey would go after presenting herself in such a raw manner.

"Check out the bod," Cassandra told the crowd, actually lifting her hands up so that her body was on full display. But she didn't stop there; she even twirled around, showing the front and the back. Her breasts weren't that big, but her ass was nice and round. It wasn't a perfect ass, but it was a good ass, a sexy womanly ass, high with a deep crack.

"You know I can't leave here tonight without singing one of Lady C's songs, a song she sang for you last week. Because I'm now completely into women, I'll have to change the lyrics a little bit, but don't worry, the song will still be hot. It'll still get the guys' dicks hard and the women wet. I promise you that. This is my rendition of 'Sweet Cheeks'. Then, I'm gonna have some lucky lady from the audience join me up here on stage."

Cassandra went into a little rap with the drummer playing behind her. She spoke/sang, rubbing a hand up and down the front of her body:

"You know you want to see it. / You know you want to kiss it. / You know you want to lick it. / You know you want to take it."

When she sang "take it," Cassandra rubbed her bald coochie and stuck a finger into the slit. She even licked her middle finger provocatively as she continued to sing.

Rickey is getting real nasty, I said to myself, as I continued to be amazed by her hot performance as the hot, funky Cassandra.

The full band played as Cassandra/Rickey rubbed her hips and sang:

"Sweet cheeks as soft as butter, / Make a grown woman scream and shudder. / Booty all naked in your Victoria's Secret shit. / Make you real wet on your clit."

The performer was non-stop sexy motion on stage as she sang:

"My lyrics are so funky and raw / That when you open my treasure / You have to explore. / Know you never had it like this. / Booty so hot, you want to give it a kiss."

That was when Cassandra stopped singing and let the music play behind her. With a sly smile, she turned to the audience and showed them her naked ass. She stood there and wiggled like she was a contestant in a Best Butt Contest. Because she had the mic in her hand, she could only use one hand to massage her own ass.

Cassandra was so much into herself that it was like she

had no time to finish the "Sweet Cheeks" song. When she turned to face us again, she put the mic back on its stand. With the mic still extremely close to her face, her tongue shot out to lick it. It looked like she was licking a dick. "I used to be real good at this," the sexy singer said, and many in the crowd laughed. Then she spoke/sang:

> *"Intoxicated by the sweet smell of my cunt, / I'm not shocking, I'm just blunt."*

But Rickey/Cassandra went beyond shocking and blunt, because at that moment, she decided to go for the goal. "Oh, baby, baby," she said as she closed her eyes. "Eat it, baby. Eat it good."

With one hand holding the mic close to her mouth, and the other hand between her smooth-looking, round thighs, she looked like a *Fox Trapper* centerfold. Because there was no hair down there, her coochie was fully exposed.

Wow! I thought. *She's going to make herself cum on that stage, in front of all these fucking people!*

The way Rickey was shaking her breasts and rubbing between her thighs made me think she was going to bust a nut.

Suddenly, her eyes snapped open wide, and putting both hands on the mic, she said, "Y'all want me to cum all over myself? Just like Lady C did when she was here, with her big, dripping pussy? I'm gonna need some help up here if y'all want me to bust one. Here's where the audience participation comes in. I want somebody to eat this pussy. This tight, dripping pussy. Any volunteers? No men allowed. All this good pussy is for the ladies. Men don't know how to eat pussy."

There were some boos from the men, but most of the audience was mesmerized by Rickey's sexy antics. She wasn't Lady Clarissa, but she had stripped down and played with herself like she was. All the things that Lady Clarissa was known for was what Rickey did. But because she didn't have any background singers, like Sallie Trim and Hallie Cum, Cassandra had to ask for a female volunteer to bring her show to its climax.

Rickey stood there with her legs spread wide and her hips pushed forward. In an ultra-sexy voice, she asked, "Who wants to eat this pussy?"

Then, she put the mic on its stand and moved to the edge of the stage. "Who wants this sweet ass?" she asked, turning around to show it all. She even reached back and pulled her cheeks apart. All she showed back there was ripe and ready. It certainly made my mouth water.

After showing that ass, she turned and showed her breasts. With a boob in each hand, she asked, "Who wants to suck on these nipples?" Her body undulated, and it was obvious she was turning herself on, moving to that crazy, sexy place of no return.

"Who...wants...to...eat...this...pussy?" Rickey asked, having some trouble getting the words out because her fingers were all up inside her.

I'm going to eat that coochie, I told myself as I moved toward the stage.

With my eyes trained on Rickey, I stood near the front of the stage. I unzipped my short jean skirt and let it slide down my long thighs. Then, I pushed it all the way down, as the crowd grew quiet behind me. I folded the skirt and neatly placed it on the edge of the stage. Then, I kicked off my mules, leaving my feet bare. The next thing to go was my white halter.

When I stepped up on the stage, I was naked, except for a pair of baby blue thongs. My ass shook as I walked, and it drove many of the guys wild, got them screaming and clapping their hands loudly. Even some of the females got loud and clapped along with the guys.

Rickey stood with her eyes closed as I walked across the stage. When she opened them, I was right there in her face. There was a look of shock and surprise on her face when she realized she was not alone. The sexy soul singer tried to step back, but I grabbed her by the wrist. I expected a tug of war because of our history, but the bold performer gave into me easily, like she had no will of her own.

It blew her mind to see me up on that stage. I almost laughed out loud. Of all the people in the world, I knew Rickey never thought she would see me. Me, Angela King, coming to take her tight, little coochie. She tried to pull away from me, but I held on tight because I didn't want to chase her all over that stage. I grabbed both her wrists and pulled her toward me. I was determined to break her ass down onstage, but I wanted to have some fun doing it.

I grabbed a wrist and opened her hand. With it open, I pulled it so that the palm hit my chest. Controlling her wrist, I rubbed her hot, little hand up, down, and beneath my breasts.

"Remember this?" I whispered as I used her hand on me.

"I don't want you up here," Rickey whispered back, looking panic stricken. "I throw out that invitation, but no one ever comes up."

"Well, I guess this is your lucky night," I replied, smirking.

"I don't want you up here," Rickey whispered again. "I just want to finish my song now."

"Lady Clarissa wouldn't back down now," I said, whispering so softly that none of the band members onstage could hear us. "You offered your coochie," I reminded her.

"Not to you. Not to you, Angela," Rickey let me know, but she made no attempt to remove her hand from between my breasts.

"Who can do it better?" I asked, while reaching behind her bareback. "Who can bust that coochie better?"

Rickey couldn't answer because that was when I reached down to grab her hot, naked ass. I stroked it and rubbed it, as she looked dead into my eyes. I knew the girl was feeling me when she bent her knees slightly, making it easier for me to rub the round curve of her ass.

Hot ass bitch, I thought, as I looked deep into her eyes and continued rubbing her ass. I even played in the crack, which made her grind her hips and moan loudly.

"I don't want you," Rickey said, and I smiled because I didn't believe her. Her nipples were hard and I could smell her arousal.

"I'm going to show you how much you don't want me," I replied, as I pushed Rickey's hand down to my belly. I pulled the waistband of my thong away from my hot skin.

"No," Rickey moaned when her hand fell into the front of my thong. "You can't make me do this."

"Make you do what?" I asked like I was innocent, real close to her face.

"You know," Rickey said, as I wedged her hand down between my skin and my thong.

"Down, Rickey," I said, standing directly in front of her. "Bring the hand down."

"Don't call me Rickey," she replied, continuing our

whispered conversation. "I hate that name."

"Bring the hand down...Rickey. Down into my wet coochie."

When I said that, Rickey's hand gripped me like a claw. She grabbed a handful, and even teased the slick folds with her middle finger. Then, she suddenly pulled her hand out of my thong, like she had just touched a hot stove. She tried real hard to resist me, but I knew once she touched my wet lips, it would bring back some sweet-ass memories. She stood there with her chest heaving, staring at me, her hand on her chest.

"Do it, Rickey. Do it," I said, while looking into her eyes.

Her hand on her chest rubbed the valley between her breasts. I knew she was at the point of no return when she brought her hand up to her lips and sniffed the finger she had stuck into my coochie.

"Do it...do it...do it," I encouraged, and Rickey began to suck her finger.

"What do you want me to do?" Rickey asked, looking so deep into my eyes that I felt she was trying to hypnotize me.

"Eat my ass," I told her as I pushed my thong down,

letting it ride low on my hips.

"Eat your ass out," Rickey said. The way she said it, it was not a question.

"Like you did at my place," I reminded her.

"I wanted to get back to you," Rickey said, tears standing her eyes like she knew she had done something wrong.

"You never came back. You never came back to get it, Rickey."

"I wanted to, Angela. I really wanted to."

"Do it now."

"I will, but if I do it…can we get together again? I want to get together again. At your place. Can we do that?"

"Yes," I told her. It made her happy, but it was a lie. As far as I was concerned, my dealings with Rickey would end on that stage.

"Pull your panties down."

"You do it," I told her. I saw no reason to make it easy for her.

I turned my back to her, and the crowd went wild. The sudden applause startled me, because for a moment, I had forgotten where I was. The crowd clapped as I turned my ass to Rickey. Then, she pushed my thong down; it became a line across my cheeks. I guess it must've looked good like that because a lot of guys hooted and stomped.

Even some females voiced their approval.

That's when I felt Rickey's hands on my hips, pulling down my thong. She pushed it all the way down, and I stepped out of them. Standing in front of her, I shuddered with excitement as she licked her tongue all the way down my back. I tingled because I knew soon Rickey's tongue would be in the crack of my ass.

Rickey used both of her hands to spread my ass cheeks. Her tongue made me squirm, but I couldn't go anyplace because she had a claw-like grip on my sweet cheeks. I let her do her thing until I couldn't take it anymore. That was when I turned around to face her. Her face was a mask of fear and excitement.

"I almost came," Rickey let me know, and then licked her lips with her long, pink tongue. In her sexiest whisper, she told me, "I almost came from eating out your sweet ass, Angela."

"I know…I know," I told her softly, as I reached out to

massage her breasts. Because they were small, I was able to cover them completely with my hands. They were small, but nicely shaped, and hot and buttery soft under my fingers.

Rickey swallowed hard and said, "Eat me. Are you gonna eat me?"

"I'm going to eat you," I informed her. Then, I lowered my hands and rubbed her hot belly.

"Thank you," Rickey said, as my hands went to her coochie.

I used one hand to open her and the other hand to stroke her clit. She was so wet and open that my fingers slid right in. Even though she was a two-faced stank bitch, I felt sorry for her. I felt like she needed this personal attention a lot more than I did. I felt that she should not be doing this in front of over a hundred people, but she had put out a challenge and I had accepted it. I was more than willing to do my part.

Her legs were spread wide as I knelt in front of her.

"Ohhhh, baby, baby," Rickey moaned when I ran my hands up the back of her thighs. "Feel so good," she sighed when I grabbed her ass cheeks. I held on to those hot buns as I let my tongue get lost inside her, digging inside the fragrant slit before my face.

Rickey screamed when she came in my mouth. Then, she bent over at the waist like someone had punched her in the belly, her orgasm exploding inside her body. I stood and watched her body jerking out of control. The crowd rocked the house with applause as Rickey suddenly straightened and threw her head back, her mouth open wide.

Still a little unsteady on her feet, Rickey reached out to me with both hands. I stepped into her arms as she wrapped them around me.

"Thank you. Thank you," Rickey said into my ear, as she held me tight to her hot body and massaged my bare ass. "Angela, I haven't come like that in a long time."

With one hand still on my ass, Rickey's other hand went up to the back of my head. She pulled me toward her and kissed me hard in my mouth, sucking on my lips, then sucking on my tongue. The deep soul kiss left me weak in the knees.

While still holding me, Rickey softly said, "I want to make you come. I want to do that for you, Angela."

I hadn't planned to take it that far on my part. My plan
was to shock Ricky, bust her coochie, and then make a quick
exit. But now that I was onstage, I thought maybe I should go for
mine. And Rickey did have that slow hand on my ass, rubbing it
like she knew how I liked it.

"Come, Angela," Rickey coaxed, trying hard to sell me on
the idea. "I know how you like to come."

I looked Rickey straight in her eyes.

"With the pussies rubbing together," Rickey told me,
speaking softly and slowly. "I'll squeeze your butt while we rub
our pussies together."

It was an offer I couldn't refuse. Still, I wasn't crazy about
lying on that dusty stage floor. However, Rickey made it easy for
me. She lay down on her back, her legs slightly spread.

The rowdy crowd went wild again, clapping and stomping
when I put my body on top of hers.

I buried my face in the sweet space between Rickey's bare
shoulder and neck. I closed my eyes and let my body fall into a
nice place between her thighs. I felt my coochie press into hers.
This is too fucking much, I thought as Rickey's clit rubbed against

mine. Very soon, she began to tremble, letting me know that she was busting another nut. When she sighed loudly in my ear, it sent me over the edge. I pushed my lower body into hers, then pressed my mouth into her neck to muffle my scream.

I came. I came hard.

It was sweet, so sweet, I thought as I held onto her.